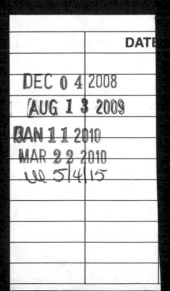

P9-DNB-151

BRINGING
THE
BOY
HOME

N. A. NELSON

BRINGING THE BOY HOME

HARPERCOLLINS*PUBLISHERS*

Library of Congress Cataloging-in-Publication Data is available.
ISBN 978-0-06-088698-1 (trade bdg.)—ISBN 978-0-06-088699-8 (lib.
bdg.)

Typography by Andrea Vandergrift
1 2 3 4 5 6 7 8 9 10
❖
First Edition

To the Nelson tribe,
for helping me through the jungle

PROLOGUE

TIRIO

My name is Tirio. I do not know who my father is. When Sara found me, I was floating down the Amazon in a *suwata curara*—a corpse canoe.

My mother had shoved the boat into the water that day. She didn't want to do it, but the choice was not hers. As a woman, she brought life into the tribe; my father, a Takunami male, made the decision of death.

"Do not be afraid," she said, cupping my chin in her hands. "It is the honorable way."

I had nodded and put on my hunting face.

"If only your body was as strong as your spirit." She ducked her head to wipe her tears and dragged the boat to the water. "But this is my fault, not yours, and I too will pay." Closing her eyes, she lifted her face to the rising sun and silently begged me not to make her ask, so I did it on my own. I shuffled over to my wooden coffin and climbed in.

The jungle was respectfully quiet, as it often is when something bigger than itself happens. And although dying is common in the rain forest, a mother sending her child to his death is not. So with its many eyes and ears, the jungle sat back and watched as Maha pushed me into the dark, whirling waters of the mighty river.

I sat cross-legged in the hollowed-out tree and lifted my chin. As the current nudged the boat away, a low-hanging branch scratched my face, but I didn't flinch. This was how I wanted her to remember me.

Deep in the forest a baby *yanuti* squawked in hunger. Its mother flew over me, shushing it with her flapping wings, but the moment was past. My moment. Maha turned and started back toward the village. It was as if I never was.

Although I was very young, I remember every detail in color. It was my sixth birthday.

My name is Tirio and I am thirteen years old. Well, almost thirteen. I was born to the Takunami tribe in the Amazon—a tribe the world knows little about. Now, more than anything, I want to go back. I want to prove to my father that I am strong enough to be a Takunami man.

LUKA

My name is Luka. I do not know who my father is. Gods willing, I will know in only a few more settings of the sun. I belong to the Takunami, the strongest people in the jungle. That is not a boast; it is the truth. The other tribes would agree if you were to ask them. How is that so? From the strongest men come the strongest offspring—and we have the strongest men. In order to become one, you must prove yourself to be powerful not only in body, but also in mind.

In our tribe, no child is told who his *paho* is until the first son of the family passes the *soche seche tente*—the sixth-sense test. Two days before I turn thirteen, I will be abandoned in the depths of the jungle with nothing but my sight, hearing, taste, touch, and smell to defend myself. Having honed these five senses since

I was born, I must trust my body to act on instinct and open my mind to the sixth sense. The father whom I have never met will send me signals. I will use these visions and voices to find my way home before the sun fully rises on my birthday.

If I fail, I will forever be banned from the village; since I have no brothers, my mother must drink tea from the *ku-ku-pa* tree and try for another son.

It has been my mother's duty to prepare me. She fed me special berries, bark, plants, and herbs given to us by the medicine man—Tukkita, the shaman. She even ate them herself when I fed from her breast. My family has made many sacrifices the past thirteen years for the promise of this new life. If I pass, all of us will benefit: my mother will be welcomed into the *urahas*, the group of women who have successfully raised a son to become a warrior; my sisters will be allowed to marry and have children of their own; and I—I will be accepted into the tribe as a warrior. As I think about how close we are to that day, I push my chest out and pull my shoulders back like the bow I hunt with. I must not fail. I am ready—ready for the test, ready to meet my paho, ready to become a Takunami man.

CHAPTER ONE

TIRIO

12 Years, 357 Days
The United States

He's going to fake left.

The boy with the number one on his jersey fakes left.

I crouch protectively in the goal area as he dribbles the soccer ball closer. With only a few minutes left, the Miami Mavericks are relying on this boy, their captain, to tie the game. Number eleven is open. Captain Maverick positions himself to pass.

"Hey!" Coach Smalley yells, flailing his arms. "Who's got eleven? Someone cover eleven!"

My best friend, Joey, steals the ball, but Captain Maverick regains control and opens himself up again.

Like a hunter trying to figure out which way his prey is going to bolt, I focus on the shift in the boy's muscles and the darting of his eyes. Is he going to pass or shoot?

His teammate, number eleven, inches closer.

5

Coach Smalley runs along the boundary line. "Left, Tirio! Watch your left!"

I start to move, but something makes me stop and step back. Captain Maverick's not going to pass.

My eyes search the boy for signs to back up my hunch. Nothing. Four boys guard him now. Eleven stands alone, waiting.

Coach is screaming at me to watch eleven.

Instead, I keep my gaze locked on the boy with the ball.

The captain faces number eleven, rears back his leg—and, at the last minute, pivots his body toward me and shoots.

Without stuttering in either direction, I catch the ball and torpedo it out of the goal area. The ref blows the whistle. Game over.

I hear Sara's signature whoop and see her standing on the bleachers, giving me a double thumbs-up. I return the gesture.

"Unbelievable." Joey runs up and high-fives me. "How did you know he was going to do that?"

I grin uneasily as my teammates slap me on the back. "I just had this feeling. It was kind of weird actually, I—"

"Weird, shmeird . . . who cares? We're going to the

championships!" he crows, throwing his arms in the air as we jog over to shake the other team's hands. "How's the foot?"

"Good." I lower my voice and look for Sara in the crowd. "I'm not even wearing my brace."

"Why not?" Joey asks. "After the way you played, Coach is gonna keep you as goalie, brace or not."

"It's not about Coach," I say as we walk toward the parking lot. "I just don't need it, that's all."

Joey gives me a sidelong glance. "If it's not about Coach, then who's it about?"

"I told you," I say, irritated. "I don't need it."

"This isn't about your dad, is it?" he asks. "About proving him wrong? He's not here to see you, T, so I don't know why you're risking getting reinjured—"

"Yeah, well, speaking of dads," I snap, "I didn't see yours in the stands."

My friend turns to look at me with a hurt expression.

Hanging my head, I regret my words. I know Joey was watching for his father the entire game. Mr. Carter's an airline pilot and although he always promises to be here, he hasn't seen Joey play once all season. "Delayed flight" or "bad weather" are the excuses he always gives.

I look up at the perfectly blue sky and bite my tongue. We've finally reached the parking lot, and Joey's mom waves at us from her car. Joey storms away.

"Hey, I'm sorry." I hurry to catch up with him. "I'm sure your dad will be here for the championships, Joe. No way he'd miss that." I grin to show him I'm not mad anymore. "And if he doesn't, who needs him? We'll win anyway, right?"

Climbing into the car, he grabs his earbuds from his backpack and puts them on. "You know what, Tirio? Maybe that's the way they do things in the Amazon, but it's not the way we do things here."

Bull's-eye. Best friends always know where to hit you the hardest.

"I'm not like them," I mumble, as Joey slams the door. "I'm not." The wind blows my words back to me like a butterfly. A pierid butterfly. *I'm not like them. . . .*

I close my eyes and my life rewinds to when I was five. My first hunting lesson with the Takunami warrior Wata. I had just pointed out a *pauq-pauq* bird that was camouflaged in the brush when Wata cupped his hand around his ear. His eyes grew big and he sprinted away, waving silently for me to follow. I loped after him but tripped over my bad foot and fell.

Trying not to cry, I untangled myself and limped toward my teacher. Fifty paces ahead, I found him staring at a flock of pale yellow pierid butterflies drinking at the river.

Without acknowledging my presence, he squatted and pulled a pierid out of the group. Holding its body gently, he plucked one wing and returned the insect to the ground. I forced myself to watch, knowing this must be a very important lesson. Gradually the forest got darker, but Wata didn't move. I bit my tongue to ignore my throbbing foot. Suddenly, the butterflies flew away, all except the pierid with the missing wing. It lay still, and I was sure it was dead.

"Wata . . ."

He silenced me with narrowed eyes. Finally he nodded. A horned frog hopped out of the forest and ogled the butterfly. The pierid fluttered frantically, but the frog jumped twice and snapped it up. Without a word, my teacher stood and started back to the village; the hunting lesson was over. I followed him and as I passed by the frog, I searched for a stick to kill it, but Wata looked back and I hurried to catch up.

Lying in my hammock that night, I couldn't sleep. Although I was excited about what I had learned, uneasiness hung over me like early morning fog. *The pierid.* Was Wata showing me that as a hunter I should go for the weakest, injured animal? Or . . . was he showing me how similar I was to the one-winged butterfly? How I too had no chance to survive in the Amazon?

Sara walks over and puts her arm around my shoulders, bringing me back to the present. "What just happened between you and Joey?" she asks, her face concerned.

"Nothing." I grab my duffel bag, throw it into the backseat of the Jeep, and climb in.

She slides into the driver's side but doesn't put the key in the ignition.

I roll down the window and lean out, letting her know I don't want to talk.

Sighing, she rummages through her tote bag at my feet and pulls out a magazine. Before she opens it, I see the cover: *Anthropology Today*. Flipping through it, she stops at a dog-eared page and tosses the magazine onto my lap.

"I brought this for you from work." She starts the car and deftly maneuvers it through the mass of vehicles trying to leave the field.

Sara teaches anthropology at the University of Miami. When she found me, she'd been living in Brazil doing research for a book, but we'd moved to Florida as soon as my adoption papers came through. She'd said three years was enough time to get the information she needed, but I think she came back here for me—for the medical treatment.

I read the title splayed across the two-page spread of the magazine: "Jungle Boys Live . . . and Die to Become Men." Six half-naked brown figures pose in front of the swirling river. The three boys in the front stand at attention, two of them wide-eyed while the third smiles slightly. Behind them, holding spears and challenging the photographer with cocked chins, stand the boys' fathers. If they didn't have the bowl haircuts of the well-known Piuchi, these men could be Takunami. I feel a stab of jealousy.

The wheels of the Jeep squeal as Sara turns onto the main road. "You've never really talked about what your tribe does . . ." She trails off. I remain quiet, knowing she won't push.

I'm right.

She nods and looks forward. "I just thought it might be interesting—with your birthday and our trip both coming up."

"Thanks," I mumble, and close the magazine. "I'll read it later." She's right; the timing is strangely coincidental. Next week Sara and I leave together for the

Amazon—her for a follow-up research expedition, me as a thirteenth-birthday present. It will be the first time either of us has been back in seven years.

We stop at a gas station to get fuel. When Sara turns off the engine and opens the door, I hear frogs croaking in the distance. Ever since that hunting trip with Wata, I've hated frogs.

Slowly, I open the magazine again.

I scan over the first page of the article. Most of it is stuff I already know: the Piuchi boys have one day—their thirteenth birthday—to track and kill a wild boar, but when I read again how they can take a bow and arrow, as well as a knife, on their quest, I shake my head. The Takunamis are only allowed the power of our bodies and minds to pass the soche seche tente. Looking down at my bad foot, I press my heel into the floorboard and flex my toes. My leg muscles pop to attention, round and strong. I tighten my quadriceps harder and, for a second, wonder what would happen if I tried to take the test now.

The gas pump clicks off and I quickly look around. I see Sara inside the store waiting in line, but no one else is nearby.

I turn the page, and what I see makes my heart stop. In the right corner of the article is a photo of a boy crouching in the dirt. He's gripping a stick and his head is bowed as if he doesn't want to be photographed. Unlike the other picture, there is no father standing behind him. The accompanying caption reads, "The boys are willing to risk injury, even death, in order to prove themselves."

The car door opens and Sara grins as she hops in. "Here." She hands me a sports drink and my favorite ice-cream bar. "A reward for my all-star goalie."

I take them from her and manage a smile. "Thanks."

"What do you think?" she asks, nodding at the open magazine and snapping her seat belt closed. "Good stuff, huh?"

"Yeah. Good stuff." I stare at the crouching boy. The photo had been cropped, so only half of him made it into the shot; he's missing an arm and a leg. I remember the pierid. I remember the horned frog. *Be strong, Piuchi boy,* I think. *I've seen what the world does to the weak. It'll eat you alive.*

LUKA

12 Years, 357 Sunrises
The Amazon

I dart glances at the men I pass, careful not to stare too long. The sky is barely even light, yet they have been gathered around the fires in front of the men's *rohacas* eating fruit and drinking *fustitu* for a while now.

Our village is built in a square, with the men's four long rohacas acting as a barrier to protect the women and children inside. We see it as the body of the warrior protecting its heart. To enter or leave the village, one must go past the men. It is a walk that both terrifies and excites me. As I make it now, some follow my passage with narrowed eyes, others watch with faces as blank as *po-no* bark, and still others ignore me completely. I pretend to search for something behind them or around them, but secretly I scan their faces for Karara's narrow nose or Sulali's fat lips. I hunt for big hands and long fingers like mine. Maha's are short and fat.

Which one is our paho? When I force myself to look

away, I cock my head to listen to their laughs and the tone of their voices. I try to remember the sound of my laugh. I watch Gimboo throw his head back and hoot at something Ruina said. Do I throw my head back like that? Or do I slap my hands as Ruina does? Both men would be great pahos, and neither of them has claimed a son.

Tonight is *Kholina*—the meeting of the married ones. I will spend the night in one of the men's straw huts while my father visits my mother. Every seven sunsets this happens. Tonight Paho will meet Maha for the last time before my soche seche tente. What will he say to her? Does he think I'm ready?

Someone grunts loudly and I snap my eyes back to the ground in front of me and hurry toward the forest. To give the paho secret away—or to try to discover the answer—is punished by death. We have seen it happen.

I shudder as I remember Luiba, the boy who snuck out the night of Kholina to listen to his parents talk. The other children and I did not even know he was gone until we heard his yelp of surprise—and then a silence so still even the jungle didn't want to break it. We never saw Luiba again. But his mother cried from one round moon to the next.

As I walked out of the hut this morning, Maha

warned me with a stern look. I nodded and grabbed my bow from its place above my hammock. I hope the grunting man won't tell her I stared too long.

When I arrive at the palm tree, I reach for the stick leaning against the trunk, poke it into the opening of the bees' nest, and stir. The air buzzes to life. Carefully, I return the stick. "Sting me." I taunt the insects as they swarm. "Sting me, winged warriors, so the aim of my arrow will be as straight as the aim of your stinger."

When I was little, I used to swat at the bees; now I stand with arms outstretched, focusing on the power each prick brings, visualizing the straight arrows I will soon shoot. Walking away, I feel myself stand taller and thank the Good Gods for providing such useful animals.

I count the tiny red bumps that have risen on my skin—twenty on one arm, nineteen on the other. I touch the ones on my chest and wonder how many my paho gets before he goes hunting.

Hearing rustling in the branches above me, I peer into the canopy and see a group of spider monkeys. I am not allowed to hunt monkeys until after I have completed my test, but I know I could get one if I tried. Banging on the base of the *wah-pu* palm, I attempt to separate one from the others. I throw a rock up and clap my hands. A big male leaps through the air and flings

16

himself to the next bough. I shake the tree to isolate him more, and it works. Screaming at me, he grabs for a vine and climbs up, lunging for a looming branch. I see my shot through an opening in the leaves. Positioning myself, I pull the bow back and point at his heart. Holding my breath and keeping my elbow close to my side, I release the string, feeling the sting of the bees in my straight aim. The empty bow twangs, and the monkey screeches and climbs higher until he is lost in the leaves.

"You are safe today," I tell him. "But next time I will use an arrow. Next time, I will take you home."

CHAPTER TWO

TIRIO

12 Years, 358 Days
The United States

I pull against the cuff that attaches my ankle to a medieval-looking machine. "How does it feel?" Dr. Riley asks.

Since Sara adopted me seven years ago, I've been coming to Sport and Health Physical Therapy to straighten and stretch my bad foot. A few beads of sweat have popped out on my forehead, but I don't flinch. "Great. I didn't feel a thing yesterday during the tournament."

He smiles. "Excellent. But you're still wearing the orthotic, right?" He wags a finger. "Don't forget to take it on your trip."

Sara clears her throat and lifts an arched eyebrow at me. I quickly look down and switch the cable to the other foot, wondering if she suspects something. "Sure," I say, trying to sound casual. "I'll take it on the trip." *But I won't wear it*, I think as I start my second set.

18

When Dr. Riley first put me on the pulley system, I was ready to bolt out the door and swim back to the Amazon. Thinking he was going to string me up, I fought like a snared animal, and it had taken several months until I finally trusted him and tried again. For two weeks, I struggled to do one repetition; now I can complete three sets of twenty.

Today I do an extra five.

"Feeling strong, huh?" Dr. Riley brings over a wobble board and points to the clock. "Three minutes. Go."

"Jeez, who in the world comes up with these things?" I step onto the square piece of wood. The design is the same as a seesaw, with the board centered on a ball underneath, and my job is to keep it balanced.

"Crap." The wood taps the floor on one side. I overcorrect. *Tap*. Then the other. *Tap*. I grit my teeth. I hate not being good at something.

"Easy, T," Sara remarks.

I take a deep breath and relax.

Dr. Riley asks Sara if we've gotten all of our vaccinations, which of course we have. Sara never slacks on that kind of stuff. She tells him about the follow-up research she's planning, and how she's looking forward to going back with me this time.

"I'll be working in the mornings," I hear her say, "but

we should still have a ton of time just to hang out and have fun. One thing I made Tirio promise is to help me find a hyacinth macaw that I can shoot."

"As in the parrot?" Dr. Riley sounds shocked. "You want to shoot a parrot?"

Sara laughs. "With my camera. And since Tirio's got such an amazing eye for spotting things, I'm sure we'll find one."

I block out their voices and focus on keeping the wobble board even. *You can do it*, I tell myself.

When I was in the Amazon, working on improving my five senses, my mother would make me repeat a task four or five times even after I'd done it correctly. "You are the weakest boy in some areas, Tirio," she had said. "Your only hope is to be the strongest in others." And then she would smile. "You can do it."

"I can do it," I mutter under my breath as the board hits the floor. "I can do it."

"Tirio?" Dr. Riley suddenly waves a hand in front of my face. "Hello? Tirio? Can you hear me?"

I stare at him, bewildered, as his words echo in my head. *Hello? Tirio? Can you hear me?*

Sara and Dr. Riley laugh as he points to his watch. "Time's up. You're good to go."

Time's up. Good to go. The voice repeats. I look at Dr.

Riley, but his mouth is no longer moving.

"What's wrong, T?" Sara asks.

I stiffen and wait for the voice to echo her words. Silence.

She comes over and helps me off the wobble board. "Tirio?"

"I'm fine," I whisper, holding my breath and looking around. "Really."

"Are you sure?" Dr. Riley hands me a bottle of water. I nod.

Sara slings my backpack over her shoulder and leads me toward the door, thanking Dr. Riley. "I think we'll just head home now," she whispers.

Head home now, the voice repeats.

I squeeze my eyes shut and wince.

"Okay—well, be careful," he says. "I'll see you soon."

Be careful . . . I'll see you soon . . . be careful.

Pushing past Sara, I run down the stairs, away from that voice—but I trip and crash onto the lawn.

Sara rushes out and helps me up. "Tirio, what's going on?"

I gulp air back into my lungs.

"Stay here with Dr. Riley," she commands. "I'll get the car."

I nod and lower myself onto a step. A fluttering in the

grass catches my eye. It's a pierid. A pale yellow pierid.
I've seen pierids in Florida, but this one is different.

"It's only got one wing," I whisper.

Dr. Riley follows my gaze. "What does?"

A strong wind catches the butterfly like a kite.

Go, go, go, my mind screams. *Get away!* But the gust
tumbles it cruelly to the end of the sidewalk, where Sara
accidentally steps on it, crushing it under her sneaker.

I can't look at the dead butterfly. I can't move. I can't
breathe.

Hello? Tirio? Can you hear me?

Time's up. Good to go.

Head home now.

Be careful. I'll see you soon.

I think the tribe that wanted me dead . . . knows
I'm alive.

LUKA

12 Years, 358 Sunrises
The Amazon

My mother looks at me expectantly.

I take a sip of the soup and list the first ingredient. "Manioc."

She grunts. That was an easy one.

"*Sawari* nuts, *ayumara* fish, *bra-bra* leaves."

Wiping sweat off the back of my neck, I scoot closer under the shadow of the thatched roof. I stare at the clothesline slung low between two poles and look for signs of a breeze. It stays as still as a dead tapir.

My mother's piercing eyes follow the bowl to my mouth as I swallow again.

"*Kha-la-mu* mushroom, *pas-puh* chile, *wu-pu* yam, and"—I make a face; it can't be—"dirt?"

My younger sister laughs and hides behind Maha. My mother smiles for a second as she looks at her daughter. "Sulali wanted to trick you by adding dirt. She thought you would never expect it."

23

"She was right." I wink at the little girl peeking out from behind Maha's arm. "I didn't expect it. Nice try, Sulali. We will see how much you like the taste of dirt later."

She screeches and jumps on Maha's back.

My mother's lips disappear into a thin line as she impatiently motions toward my soup. "Continue."

"Palm fruit, *manala* root, vanilla, *conto* weed, and"—I drain the bowl and place it on the ground triumphantly—"frog eggs."

Maha frowns. Sulali jumps down and stares with wide, expectant eyes.

"You must tell me more," Maha demands.

"More? Maha, that was all. There is nothing more."

"You must be specific."

My older sister, Karara, has just returned from the garden. Placing her woven basket on the ground, she cocks her hips and smirks. Sulali moves away from Maha and grabs Karara's hand. I look at the basket overflowing with manioc root and go over everything in my head. What did I miss? A new spice? A rare leaf? Ants? I am sure of my list and look up. Karara rolls her eyes. I glare at her. Sulali bites her lip, and Maha's face is blank. To help me now would only harm me later.

24

They will not be in the jungle in four days to give me answers, so they do not now.

Karara picks the basket up and turns to go inside.

"*Kupu-kupa* frog eggs, the silver tree frog," I shout triumphantly at her back. She flicks her wrist over her head to show she is not impressed and disappears into our hut. I turn toward my mother and her face relaxes into a smile.

"Yes," she says, patting my head. "Tomorrow we test your ears."

"Maha?" I stand, knowing if I don't ask my question now, I will lose my courage. "Last night at Kholina, when you saw Paho . . ."

She narrows her eyes.

"Did he . . ." I fumble for the words I practiced. "Do you think . . ."

"Yes?" she snaps.

"Is he happy with where I am?" I blurt. "With my progress? Does he think I'm ready?"

"He will be happier when you have passed," she says, turning away. "And so will I."

We hear Karara snort.

Maha freezes in midstep and slowly curls her hands into fists. Spinning around, she smiles widely at Sulali and me.

25

"Yes, Luka," she announces loudly. "Your paho is very proud of you . . . his *son*."

I walk over to the wash pot. "Good," I murmur, dipping my soup bowl in and swirling it around.

There is silence from inside our hut.

CHAPTER THREE

TIRIO

12 Years, 358 Days
The United States

" I feel fine," I assure Sara as we walk toward Cal's diner. "Really." I hold open the restaurant door and realize I'm still shaking. "I think I just need something to eat. Plus, didn't it seem really hot in Dr. Riley's office?"

Sara looks concerned as she walks inside. "Not particularly." She pauses, then adds, "I wouldn't want you to be sick for our trip, Tirio. We can always postpone it, if we need to."

From behind the counter Cal's face lights up when he sees us, and he waves. "How are my favorite two customers today?" he asks as we sit down at our usual spot.

"Starving," I say. Cal chortles as he ladles soup into a huge bowl and slides it toward me with a sly grin. "You will never get this one," he whispers. "Never. If you get it right, free soup for the rest of the year."

For the past five years, Sara and I have been coming to Cal's Gourmet Diner after my physical therapy sessions. This tradition started when Cal and I developed an unusual friendship over his famously secret soups. All of Cal's recipes come out of his head; he never uses a cookbook and he won't tell anyone the ingredients. People beg him, even offer him cash, but he always refuses.

I would silently cheer every time he turned someone down, happy that I wasn't the only one hiding something.

When I was eight, I decided to share my secret with Cal.

"Almonds, cauliflower, cucumber, yogurt," I said.

Cal stopped cutting the tomatoes.

"Garlic, beef broth, dill . . ."

He walked over to where Sara and I were sitting and crossed his meaty arms on the counter.

"And pepper." I smiled shyly and looked down.

"How in the world?"

"What did he do now?" Sara laughed.

"I think you've got a future chef on your hands."

"Why, is he giving you hints on how to improve your soup?"

"What do you mean? My soup is perfect." Cal clutched his chest in mock offense but continued to look at me with admiration. "No, this young man just listed all the ingredients in his soup. Every single one."

Sara whooped. "Really. Well, maybe Tirio and I should open a restaurant across the street and give you a run for your money, Cal."

Leaning down so we were eye to eye, he stroked his mustache and stared at me seriously. "Mr. Tirio," he said, "come back next Friday and I will make a new soup for you. But next time, young man, could you whisper the ingredients in my ear?"

I looked at his hairy ears and grimaced.

He threw back his head and laughed. "Or write them down, if you wish. As remarkable as your talent is, sir, I do not want my recipes advertised for everyone to hear, you see?"

I nodded solemnly. I didn't want to be the one to ruin his secret.

Five years later, as Sara and I sit in the same seats, he's still trying to stump me. Sometimes I get them wrong, but often I'm right—especially lately. I've been on a roll.

"Go for it, Mr. Tirio." He smiles today. "This one is especially tough, so take your time. Let me know when you're ready."

I sip a spoonful. A familiar taste hits my tongue and

my stomach flip-flops. "Oh my God."

"What?" Sara rummages through her tote bag and pulls out a pen. "Did he make it really spicy? You're not going to be sick, are you?"

Shaking my head, I grab the pen from her and begin writing on my napkin.

Chicken broth

Lime

Cilantro

Pepper

Chicken

Sorengi mushrooms

Paprika

Worcestershire sauce

Basil

Salt

My hand is shaking as I write down the last ingredient. Although I haven't eaten it in seven years, I would know this taste anywhere.

Manioc

Sara gives a low whistle as she peers over my shoulder. "Where in the world did Cal get manioc?"

I shrug, and although my heart is pounding, I try to act nonchalant as I give the napkin to Cal.

The older man shakes his head in disbelief and then

holds out his hand in congratulations. I shake it and go through the motions of shrugging and grinning sheepishly, but inside my mind is screaming, *Manioc!* I ate manioc twice a day when I lived in the jungle, but I haven't had it once since I've been here. And in Cal's diner? My mind churns with questions. *Why would Cal put it in my soup?*

During the drive home, an eerie feeling settles over me. The hunch on the soccer field. The strange voices. The appearance of the manioc. *What does it all mean?*

When we pull into the driveway, I still don't have any answers.

"So how do you feel now that you've eaten?" Sara asks as she unlocks the front door of our townhouse. "Better?"

I drop my backpack under the enormous palm tree that has overtaken the small hallway. Not wanting her to postpone our trip, I manage what I hope is a convincing smile. "One hundred percent better."

She stares at me with narrowed eyes, unsure. So I lift my arms and flex my muscles like a bodybuilder, making different grimacing faces with each pose.

Finally, she laughs. "Okay, okay, I get it. Save the impression session for Juan Diego. He already told me the dining hall at the camp needs a new roof. One look at you, and he'll have you up there with a hammer and nails."

Juan Diego is one of Sara's oldest friends. He's a Brazilian ethnobotanist and was driving the boat the day Sara found me floating in the corpse canoe. He's still working at the research camp.

I straighten up so that I'm almost as tall as Sara. "I could do it."

"I know," she says. "And you probably will." Sara starts flipping through the mail. "Oh, by the way, Professor Goodwin is coming over later, probably around eight. . . ."

"Professor Goodwin, huh? You mean tall, dark, handsome"—I put my arm around a wooden spider monkey sculpture sitting on the hall table—"*single* Professor Goodwin?"

"He offered to teach my classes while I'm away." Sara doesn't look up, but a smile has crept onto her face. "And he wants to discus my syllabus."

"Good thing we just cleaned the house and there are fresh flowers on the table," I say, following her into the kitchen.

"What I'm trying to get at," Sara continues, ignoring my taunts, "is that the rest of the week is very busy and I'd like to wrap the gifts we're taking to the research camp before he gets here. Can you help?"

I shrug my shoulders. "Sure."

"Thanks." She motions toward the living room. "There's a bag of stuff in there. Why don't you bring it into the kitchen, so we'll have more room."

I walk through the archway of Kai'inga hunting spears into our living room. All around me are reminders of Sara's work as an anthropologist. Masks of warriors leapfrog with photos of Sara and me on our annual camping trip. A hollowed-out honey-colored gourd sits between last year's soccer trophy and a lopsided clay vase I made Sara for Mother's Day. Even the windows are decorated with woven reed blinds pulled up by braided vines.

"Tirio," Sara calls.

I pick up the bag and take it into the kitchen, where we start sorting through the gifts Sara bought. There's a bunch of stuff for the American staff at the camp, as well as some small toys for the kids in the local tribes.

"What are you looking forward to the most?" Sara asks as she tapes up a box of paperback mysteries the camp cook likes. "With our trip, I mean. The river? The animals? More manioc?"

I peel the price tag off a wooden puzzle and consider her question. "Things normal Takunami boys do," I admit, a little embarrassed to be saying the words out loud.

"*Normal* Takunami boys?" Sara asks, surprised. She glances up at me. "What kind of things do you mean?"

I pause for a minute, recalling the sight of my tribe-mates sprinting full force toward the river as they raced to be the first ones in. I think about how I used to pound on a hollow wooden bucket while the other kids learned the Takunami hunting dances, and how I used to sit at the base of the kapok tree while they climbed and tried to reach the sky.

"Climb a kapok tree," I finally say.

"A kapok," she repeats.

I nod slowly, knowing what she's thinking: the kapok is one of the tallest trees in the Amazon. "I want to do it all," I say. The determination comes out in my voice as I realize the possibilities. "I want to do everything I couldn't do before."

"Okay," Sara says quietly. "Then that's what we'll do."

As we sit together, wrapping the gifts, Sara chatters on about how much she's looking forward to getting away from the traffic in the city and how she can't wait to see all her old friends again. I nod and pretend to listen, but in my mind, I'm still thinking about my answer: *I want to do it all.*

The doorbell rings and while Sara quickly puts everything away, I let Professor Goodwin in. Pretending to be exhausted from physical therapy, I say good night and haul my backpack upstairs. In truth, I want to be alone just as much as they do. I need to think.

Crawling under the covers, I curl up onto my side and close my eyes. In the darkness, with only the murmur of voices below me, I am transported back to when I was a little boy in the jungle, lying in a hammock—squeezing my eyes shut and praying to the Good Gods to make me normal overnight. To help me run, dance, and climb.

My prayers have been answered. My foot is better. I've been able to do everything a normal boy does. Everything a normal *American* boy does. But aren't I a Takunami? I think about all the things that have been happening the past few days. Why now—a week before my thirteenth birthday? A week before I'm supposed to go back to the Amazon? There's only one reason that I can think of.

When I realize what I'm considering, I roll over onto my back and stare up at the rotating blades of the ceiling fan. *Could I do it? Could I really take the test?*

Downstairs Sara laughs loudly, and my mind skids to a halt. I sit up. I can't leave Sara. And even though she studies jungle tribes for a living, she would never let me take such a dangerous test. But the weight of this opportunity punches me in the gut—the chance to finally prove my father wrong—and I pull my knees into my chest.

I have to go. Somehow, I'll have to sneak out of our cabin in the Amazon and make my way back to my village. Alone. But maybe if I leave a note for Sara, at least she'll know where I've gone and why I'm doing what I need to do.

Hopping out of bed, I switch on my desk lamp and pull out a sheet of paper. I can't sleep now, so I begin to write:

Dear Sara,

A couple of days before we left on this trip, you asked me what I was looking forward to the most about going back. And I told you that I wanted to do things normal Takunami boys do, remember? Well, there's one other thing that every normal Takunami boy does, and as you read this, I'm on my way to make that happen. I'm going back to my village to take my soche seche tente. I promise to come

back as soon as I'm finished. Don't
worry. I'll be fine.

I hear footsteps downstairs. Sneaking over to my door, I crack it open and see Sara and Professor Goodwin standing in the hallway. He's got his jacket on, which means that he's leaving. Sara cautiously peers around the huge palm tree and looks up toward my room. I jerk my head back behind the door and hold my breath. I hear her laugh softly and then Professor Goodwin's low baritone. The front door clicks closed, and after a minute of silence, I hear glasses being put into the sink. Knowing she'll be coming to bed soon, I tiptoe over to the backpack lying on the floor, fold the note in half, and hide it in the back inside pocket. I'll finish it later.

As I turn off the desk light and climb into bed, I think of the last two lines I wrote.

Don't worry. I'll be fine.

A sudden chill runs through my body. Takunami boys, no matter how strong, never make that promise.

LUKA

12 Years, 359 Sunrises
The Amazon

"Karara, weave the *wah-pu* into baskets, crush up the *ay-ah-e-yah*—the men need more for fishing tomorrow—and watch your sister. I'm taking Luka to the forest." My mother fires out the orders and, without waiting for a reply, heads down the path.

"Anything else?" my sister shouts. "Should I cook Luka's lunch, or oil his bow?"

Whether my mother doesn't hear, or just chooses to ignore Karara, I don't know. Looking back at my sister, I wince and mouth, *Sorry*. She shoots me a venomous look and, with a flip of her long black braid, turns and starts pounding the ay-ah-e-yah root with such force, I wonder if there will be any left for fishing.

As the firstborn daughter of a Takunami family, life has been put on hold for Karara. For the past fifteen years, she has not known our father either—and *will not* until I pass my test. Because Maha has focused all her energy on me, Karara has taken over the mothering of Sulali.

It will be over in a couple of days, I assure myself.

"Karara has grown into a beautiful woman," I say, rushing to catch up with my mother.

"Not with that sour expression she always wears, and beauty is nothing if you are lazy. No man will want to marry her if she continues to complain all the time."

I drop the subject, but continue to think about my sister. She will certainly have no problem finding a husband. And she is definitely not lazy. No, the word I would use to describe Karara is *spirited*. Where most women in our tribe cut their hair short because it is easier to keep clean, my sister has only cut hers twice. She uses oil from the tonka nut so it shines blue-black in the sun, and she fixes it differently every day. When it is not braided, it flows down her back, rippling like the Amazon itself. Some of the women look at her disapprovingly, but Karara doesn't seem to care and Maha is too busy with me to notice.

"Luka, come here." My mother unties a piece of cloth from around her waist and covers my eyes. "Whenever you hear a sound—any sound, no matter how small—I want you to tell me what it is."

I see white stars behind the darkness of my eyelids. "Maha, the cloth is too tight," I complain.

She yanks the knot tighter. "Stop talking for once and listen."

A bird flies overhead. Two flaps. Long wings. Solid landing. "Harpy eagle," I whisper.

Our still bodies are now shadows, invisible unless we move or speak. The jungle has been holding its breath since we walked in; but as it accepts us, little puffs of sound are released until it's so loud, I can barely focus on one noise before another takes over.

A rustling to my right. A pause. The rustling continues, muffled as it moves below the damp, rotting leaves. "*Bedenga* lizard."

Tap-tap-tap. "Woodpecker . . . redheaded woodpecker."

Mweh, mweh. "*Kah-mo* bird."

Poo-poo-poo. "Capuchin monkey."

Drip. Surely she doesn't want me to say what that is. I identify it just in case. "Raindrop."

As the jungle comes at me from all directions, I feel vulnerable being blindfolded and crouch down. "*Ka-ka* frog, *mar-al* toucan, howler." I spit out the names quickly. As I say one, fifteen more spring into my head, layering my brain: floor dwellers sink to the bottom, followed by the inhabitants of the belly of the forest, then the residents of the chest of the forest, and lastly those that live in the head. "*Kono-paku, simbo-kallu, kancho spider.*"

I hear the pounding gallop of a tapir charging toward us. These piglike creatures are not dangerous, but we are standing in a curve of the path, so it will not see us in time to stop or even swerve. "Tapir!" I warn, diving into the jungle. It whizzes by me and I feel its coarse hair graze my leg.

"Tambo!" Maha yells.

Tambo? Our pet? I whip off the blindfold and leap up, brushing the rotted *kamana* leaves off my leg. My mother stomps back toward the village and I run after her. Halfway home, we see Sulali skipping toward us, flinging a stick into the air and humming.

"Sulali." My mother speaks through clenched teeth.

Looking up, my sister's face breaks into a smile. "Maha. Luka." She races toward us.

"What are you doing out here?" Maha asks.

Sulali stops, and her five-year-old face crumples. "Going swimming with Tambo."

41

"Where is Karara?"

My sister looks down and shrugs. Maha grabs Sulali's elbow and continues toward home. Tambo has returned, looking for his swimming partner, and nibbles at our ankles with his trunklike snout. Maha kicks him and he yelps in surprise. Sulali starts to cry, but my mother ignores her. I desperately try to think of a way to warn Karara of our arrival.

Although our hut is very close to the entrance of the village, we must walk past the men's rohacas to reach it. Some of the warriors smirk as Maha strides by. We approach our cooking fire and I see my oldest sister speaking with our neighbor, Metuta. The handsome boy pokes the wood as Karara stirs a pot and laughs at something he says.

Maha hands Sulali to me. "Go to the garden and dig up some *patj-kam* root."

My younger sister protests but stops midhowl when she sees me press my middle three fingers against my lips and widen my eyes in silent warning.

"Luka . . . ," she whines.

"Don't worry, Sulali. I won't let anything happen." I sneak a look over my shoulder and watch my mother grab a piece of dried bamboo and approach Karara. I push Sulali behind me.

"Stay here," I order. "Don't move."

As I turn back around, I watch my mother raise the stick.

"No!" I scream.

My cry is lost in the whistle of the bamboo as it sings through the air and smacks against my sister's back. Karara yelps and spins around. Metuta shields his face with his arms and stumbles away, but my mother ignores him and whips the bamboo down again. Karara clenches her jaw as her arm begins to bleed and tries to grab the stick.

Sulali sprints past me. "No! Don't hit her, Maha." She darts between the two women and tries to push them apart, just as my mother swings again.

With a hollow thud, Sulali crumples to the ground, blood pouring from her nose. She doesn't move. I race toward her.

Karara drops to her knees. "Are you okay, Sulali? I'm so sorry. Wake up, little one, wake—"

Whack! The bamboo cracks down on Karara's back with such force that she falls on top of Sulali. I grab my mother's arm.

"Stop, Maha! Enough!"

She whips around, and spit flies on my face as she seethes. "No one is going to stop you from passing your test. No one!"

CHAPTER FOUR

TIRIO

12 Years, 359 Days
The United States

"Hey Joe, how's it going?" I stand my bike against his porch stairs and lower myself into an old rocker.

Creak, creak. The wood objects as I lean backward. The sound is so piercingly clear, I wince and bend forward.

Grooooan. The faded porch complains.

Joey keeps reading.

I'm getting impatient. I've come over to tell Joey about my decision to take the soche seche tente, but he still hasn't forgiven me for what I said about his father. Rubbing my eyes, I exhale loudly. First things first.

"The reason I said what I did about your dad . . ." I search for words that will make things better. "It's just . . ."

Joey glares at me.

It doesn't matter what I say; he'll only defend his father anyway. "I was mad about what you said about my orthotic—and my dad—so I just lashed out. I'm sorry."

Joey shrugs, but his face has relaxed. "You got mad because you know it's true, T," he says. "You're always saying that you want to prove him wrong. But just because you're angry at your dad doesn't mean you need to take it out on mine." He turns back to his magazine. "Besides, he promised me things would change soon. He's switching his flight schedule so we can spend more time together."

Joey turns the page, and the sound is like the crash of a wave upon the shore. I lean forward and cover my ears.

"Now that's just rude," Joey says.

I clench my jaw.

Chirp-chirp. A brown chickadee beckons and I lift my head toward the yard, searching for the source of the sound. *Chirp-chirp. Flap-flap.* It flies away from the oak tree. Joey follows my gaze, his eyes hunting for whatever it is I'm looking at.

"What?" he asks.

"Can't you hear it?" I whisper. "The bird? The turning of the page?"

Pschhhhhh. Someone a block away opens a can of soda.

"The soda can?" I sit frozen, waiting for the next sound. Joey cocks his head.

Leave a message after the beep. Beep. An answering machine clicks on in the house behind the Carters'.

Joey looks at me like I'm crazy. "What are you talking about?"

"Some really weird stuff's been happening to me the last couple days, Joe." I try to block out the sounds around me and focus on what I have to say.

"Like what?"

I start listing the week's events. "First, I could feel that Captain Maverick was going to kick and not pass the other day—*feel* as in knew without a shadow of a doubt, like I could read his mind—and then I heard voices during PT. . . ."

Joey scrunches up his face. "You're hearing voices? Did they tell you to say that mean stuff about my dad, too?"

I ignore his comment and continue. "And then I saw a pierid butterfly with only one wing, and at Cal's I ate manioc for the first time in seven years."

Joey has already gone back to reading.

Click, click, click, click. Inside the house, the gas under a burner ignites.

"Your mom just turned on the stove," I tell Joey.

He rolls his eyes.

"Go check."

"Okay, Houdini." Joey stands. "I'll play your game."

The hinges squeak dryly as he opens the screen door. Now that I expect the sounds, they don't bother me.

"Hey, Mom?" he calls. "What are you doing?"

"Fixing lunch," she yells back. "Does Tirio want to stay? I'm making grilled cheese."

Without answering her, he pulls the door shut and sits back down opposite me.

"How'd you know that?" He sounds suspicious, but also ready to listen.

"I heard it," I say. "I know this all seems weird to you, Joey, but I think I'm being called back to the Amazon."

"Called back to the Amazon?" Joey repeats. "That's insane. By who?"

"My father."

Joey turns red in the face. "Is this your idea of a joke?" he asks. "First you take a jab at me because my dad didn't make it to the game, and now you're telling me *your* father—who thinks you're dead—is calling you home?"

47

"It has to be him, Joe. He's the only one that can communicate with me this way."

"Yeah, well, what about the butterfly and the manioc? Is your father some kind of Amazonian magician who can just wave his hand and—poof—make them appear?"

I shake my head. "Actually, I think they're signs from the Good Gods. They're the ones who control the spirits of plants and animals. My father has no power over them."

"Good Gods? T, you've really lost it this time." He pauses, and then adds cautiously, "Why would they be calling you back anyway?"

I lift a finger to my lips and tentatively hold my breath, listening. The refrigerator door slams and I hear Mrs. Carter humming as a jar pops open. She's still in the middle of fixing lunch; she's not going to interrupt us. I shake my head, grateful that my skills work when I want them to.

I pull out the *Anthropology Today* magazine from my backpack. Opening it to the dog-eared article, I hand it to him. "My thirteenth birthday is coming up, you know. Take a look at this."

He quickly scans the article and widens his eyes as he looks up at me. "Are you saying your dad and these Good Gods of yours want you to take this test?"

"Not *that* test exactly," I say, shaking my head. "The soche seche tente. It's the Takunami version of a manhood test. In order to pass, I'd have to find my way through the jungle and back to our village, with my father using the sixth sense to guide me."

He raises an eyebrow. "You're not going to try to do it, are you?"

I look him straight in the eye and nod slowly. "Yes. But I'm not going to accept his help."

"Why not? Because you think he might try to kill you again?"

"No." I cross my arms over my chest. "Because I want to do it *alone*."

He sits bolt upright. "What?"

"I just want to prove to my dad that I'm not the useless weakling he thought I was," I say, lowering my voice. "When I left the Amazon, I gave up on ever taking my soche seche tente, but now that my foot's better—"

"With a little help from modern medicine," he interrupts.

"—and Sara and I are going back for my birthday, and now these signs . . ." I shake my head in disbelief. "He's calling me back, Joe. He knows I'm alive. This is my chance."

Joey stares at me. "Not wearing your orthotic is one

thing, Tirio," he says. "But going back to a tribe that tried to kill you, just to prove a point, is another. Even if I do want my dad to be around more, I wouldn't stand in front of his plane to keep it from taking off to make that happen."

I hear the soft slapping of bare feet on the hardwood floor. "You're mom's coming," I warn him.

We both turn just as the door opens.

"Hey, Tirio." Mrs. Carter smiles. "Can you stay for lunch?"

I nod. "Sure, thanks."

She motions us in. "The food's in the kitchen, but you boys can eat out here, if you'd like."

Joey storms past her into the kitchen, snatches a plate of sandwiches and pickles from the table, and stomps back outside.

I take the other plate and rush after him.

"Don't forget your drinks!" Mrs. Carter calls as she grabs the cordless phone.

I see the two glasses of ice tea sitting on the counter. Hurrying outside, I set my plate down and then run back to get the tea.

I grab one glass. *Scratch, scratch*. A cat sharpens its claws on a tree in Havana Park.

I grab the other. *Tick, tick, tick, tick.* Someone's watch ticks off seconds in the bathroom.

I head for the porch but freeze when I hear Mrs. Carter's voice. "This weekend," she murmurs to someone on the phone upstairs. "Stan's flying in, and we're going to tell him together."

There's a pause and then Mrs. Carter starts crying softly.

"Joey's going to blame himself," she says. "I know he will. He'll think the divorce is his fault, like maybe there was something he could have done to prevent it, but"—she gulps in a breath—"this is my fault, not his. . . ."

A wind blows in through the open sliding door and whispers behind me:

my fault, not his
  my fault, not his
    my fault, not yours

I spin around and come face to face with my mother. Not Sara, but Maroma—my Takunami mother. Brown and dusty, she hasn't changed since the last time I saw her, from her slight smile to her haphazard haircut.

A fly lands on her forehead and she brushes it away. *"This is my fault, not yours, and I too will pay,"* she repeats. *"I too will pay."*

I drop one of the glasses and it shatters on the tile floor. I look down and see slivers of glass sparkling up at me as tiny drops of blood appear on my foot.

When I glance up again, Maroma is gone.

Mrs. Carter rushes downstairs.

Outside! my mind yells. I don't want her to know what I heard.

Thump, slide, thump, slide. I recognize the sound instantly. I'm dragging my foot. I haven't done that for years.

Maha.

I slam the lone glass of tea onto the picnic table and lean over the porch railing, gasping for breath.

"What's wrong?" Joey asks.

"What happened?" Mrs. Carter is standing in the doorway, looking nervous.

"I accidentally dropped a glass," I say, composing myself and turning around. "I'm sorry, Mrs. Carter. I'll clean it up." I head toward her, dragging my foot with me.

Mrs. Carter's gaze drops down to my leg. "Did you hurt yourself?"

"No, my foot's just acting up again."

"Don't worry about it, Tirio," she says. "I'll do it."

She pauses, then turns to Joey. "Honey, your father's coming home this weekend. Don't make any plans for Saturday night; he wants us all to go out for dinner."

Joey's face lights up. "Really? Cool! Can we go to Las Conchitas?"

"Sure," she says, smiling tightly as she closes the heavy wooden door. "I'll make reservations."

Joey's almost trembling with excitement when he looks at me. "Ha. Told you things were going to change." He laughs as he takes a bite of his sandwich. "So, what really happened in there?"

Not wanting to spoil his happiness—and knowing he won't believe me anyway—I decide not to tell him about what the "change" really means. "I saw a vision of my mother," I answer, my voice even.

Joey doesn't even bother to doubt me anymore, as if his father coming this weekend makes everything possible. "Sara?" he asks.

"My Takunami mother."

He stops chewing for a second, and looks confused. "If the Good Gods control the plants and animals, and your father controls you, who controls your mother?"

"I told you," I say through clenched teeth. "My father doesn't control me. Or my mother." Staring down at my bad foot, I push away from the railing. My foot feels strong. I take a step. It holds me. I take another and another, until I'm standing next to Joey. "I need your help." I narrow my eyes. "I need you to help me prepare for a two-day trip in the Amazon jungle."

LUKA

12 Years, 360 Sunrises
The Amazon

"Today we test your eyes," my mother says.

My heart quickens as I stare at the sight in front of me.

"Caiman, peccary, fer-de-lance, jaguar, and anteater." Maha pauses in front of each of the five forms. "You must find every one by nightfall."

She has gone too far. She has involved others.

"Maha, these boys aren't old enough to stay out all day. They're still children; not one of them is over six." I watch five little chests poke out further and five chins lift higher in response to what I said.

Ignoring me, she smudges ash on the arm of the fer-de-lance snake, Kapuki. "The boys will not make sounds, so you must rely on your eyes alone. These are all animals that can harm you in your journey home."

The young boys, serious and determined in their camouflage, follow Maha's every move with their eyes.

Their bodies have been meticulously decorated to mimic the skin, scales, or fur of each creature: *ru-pah* leaf to change Luwta's brown skin to the black-green of a caiman; *atuh* berry and ash on Kapuki to duplicate the pattern of the deadly fer-de-lance snake; *lustu* root on Pisteru to look like the fur of the anteater; real peccary hairs attached to Weru's back; and Kiwano, the youngest of the group at four years old, painted with *u-shuh* berry and *rioba* sap to look amazingly like a miniature jaguar.

I run my fingers through my hair. "What if something happens to them? I do not want to be responsible."

"They will be in their natural habitats." Maha continues pacing. "In other words, the peccary will be on the ground, not in a tree."

Pisteru giggles until Weru, the peccary, shoots him an angry look. At six, Weru is the fattest of the boys and a poor climber. I am sure that is why he was chosen as a ground animal.

"The caiman and jaguar might be on land *or* water, and the fer-de-lance might be in a tree or on the ground. They will all be two hundred footsteps from the wash area."

"What if I do not find them by nightfall?"

She ignores me. "When you spot one, give the call of the *tooka* bird and say the name of the animal. The boy will award you with a seed from the sho-ro sho-ro bush, which you will then put in this." She holds up a small leather pouch. "Once you have all five seeds, you may return to the village."

"What do the boys do when I find them?"

My mother slowly narrows her eyes at me. "My son, for someone who in three sunrises is supposed to have all the answers, you ask a lot of questions." She hands me the pouch and then jerks her head toward the forest. The five boy-animals silently race toward the jungle. "Stay here until the sun has reached midsky and then you can begin," she instructs me before striding away. I stare after her helplessly.

"It looks like someone has something to prove," a deep, soft voice behind me says.

Surprised, I turn and see Tukkita, the Takunami shaman, standing under the shade of the po-no. His tiny, wrinkled body is dwarfed by the tree's massive trunk.

"Oh, and I will, Tukkita," I assure the medicine man, my voice sounding louder than I intended.

He closes his eyes and I swallow a lump in my throat.

Was my tone disrespectful? I look down. "The boys will be fine and I will prove myself."

"That is something we will find out in a few days, my proud friend," he says, shuffling away, "but it is not you I was talking about."

As the sun moves upward, I walk to the shade of the po-no tree where Tukkita had been standing.

It is not you I was talking about. The shaman's words repeat in my head. If not me, then who? It couldn't be the boys; they are just following Maha's orders. So it had to be . . . *Maha?* The papaya I had for breakfast churns in my stomach and the acid works its way up my throat as I lean over and rest my hands on my knees.

Tukkita said what everyone else is thinking. As hard as I try to ignore the raised eyebrows and whispers of the other villagers, it is difficult when Maha parades me around after the completion of each test.

It is true that no other Takunami mother has ever gone through such widespread testing to prepare her son for his soche seche tente. But Maha is just that type of person. Everything she does is beyond what is necessary. When she makes a piece of clothing, she folds the jagged edges over to make a straight hem. When

58

she cooks, she adds extra spices. I watch her stay busy until late in the night, and when I wake, she has already begun another project. Sometimes I look for signs that she has slept at all.

When she is happy, she is very happy. When she is mad, she is crazy mad. But I have come to accept it as the way Maha is. Now Tukkita's words plant doubt. What does my mother have to prove?

"Luka," a small voice says. I straighten up and see Sulali. I grimace at her two black eyes and swollen nose. She was passed out for half of yesterday after being hit with the bamboo.

"You are a sight, little one." I sit down and pull her to me.

She giggles and wiggles into my lap. Growing quiet, she opens my hand and grabs the leather pouch. I wait for her to speak and notice how long her hair has gotten. Karara has braided it identically to hers for the past couple of weeks. I'm sure Maha hasn't noticed.

"Do good, Luka," she finally says. "Do good, so Paho can come live with us. Do good, so Maha and Karara will be happy."

My whole body sags. Karara is not the only sister who has suffered from my training.

"Paho will not ever live with us, Sulali," I remind her softly. "Even after I pass the test, he must stay in the men's rohacas."

Her chin trembles, and I stop myself from telling her that I too will be moving there.

"But he can play with you every day." I clap her hands together. "And spin you around a lot higher than I can, I'm sure."

She sniffs. "Really?"

"So high you will be saying *eh-eh* to the *muwipa*."

She giggles.

I hug my sister. "Now go find Tambo and cause some trouble."

She buries her head in my shoulder.

"Go, before I make you eat dirt like you made me." I grab some soil and she shrieks and jumps up.

"*Kuiju*—I love you." Her eyes flit to mine for a second and then dart back to the ground.

It is not something my family says, and I wonder where she heard it. I tug at the bottom of her skirt and peer up at her face. "Kuiju, Sulali. We all do—very much; Paho also. You will see. Very soon this will all be over and we will be a happy family."

My sister smiles and I force myself to laugh. "Now get out of here, before Maha catches you."

"Good luck," she whispers.

I push her gently. "Go."

As she skips away, I notice the shadow of the po-no tree has disappeared. Taking a deep breath, I stand, tie the cinched pouch to my wrist, and head toward the wash area.

The coolness of the jungle instantly puts me at ease, and the load on my shoulders lifts with each step. "Hello, old friend." I smile. The leaves nod as I pass, and patches of light speckle the path, pulling me forward. I jump from one patch to the other and think again of Sulali.

I must do well.

Upon reaching the clearing that opens onto the river, I search for any signs that one of the boys might be hiding in the water. No such luck. I guess this isn't going to be that easy after all.

Last season, flooding destroyed our wash area and the men worked for five days to build a new one. They wove river reeds together to form a circular fence that reaches twenty paces into the river and also twenty paces along the shore. It is the only place where our tribe can safely bathe, clean our clothes, and swim. The gate we enter through is always closed to keep the caimans out, but I notice now, with some unease, that it is open.

Hurriedly I shut it, wrapping the leather straps around the top and bottom of the door. Peering into the water again, I look for a pair of reptile eyes, but see nothing.

Setting my jaw, I go over my plan. Starting by the water's edge, I will walk two hundred steps into the forest and then come back, combing the area in a fanlike pattern. It should only take me a few hours. I shake the gate to make sure it stays closed, recheck the river, and begin.

After walking about a hundred steps, I gag and stumble backward. Covering my nose, I breathe out of my mouth until I come upon a tree bearing the horrible-smelling but delicious *ah-ku-de* fruit. Passed out against the trunk is Weru, the boy assigned to be the peccary. Staring at him—with his hands clasped across his chubby belly and sweet, slimy pulp all over his face—I shake my head and decide to teach him a lesson.

I step behind another tree and mimic the call of the *tooka* bird softly. *"Wee-wee-o."*

Weru doesn't stir.

"Wee-wee-o." A little louder this time.

He shifts and rolls to his side.

I repeat the call once more and Weru stiffens. I can see him searching for me but trying not to move. I have yet to call out the name of an animal, so he doesn't know if I have spotted him or someone else.

"White-lipped peccary," I finally say, and appear from behind the tree. His peccary hairs have come unglued and hang pitifully down his back. Slowly he stands and, without meeting my gaze, hands over the sho-ro sho-ro seed.

"Go wash off, Weru. The flies and mosquitoes will have you for supper if you don't."

Hunched over, he shuffles toward the water.

"Oh, and Weru, make sure to close the gate. Someone left it open earlier."

He freezes.

"Was it you?" I ask.

He shakes his head.

"It's okay," I assure him. "Go. The flies have already found you."

He casts a fearful glance at the water. "Better the flies have me for dinner than a caiman, Luka."

"There are no caim—" But he is already jogging away. I wipe the ah-ku-de pulp off the seed and slip it into the pouch.

Two hours later, I have found all the boys except one. Kiwano, the four-year-old jaguar, is still missing. Thunder claps in the distance; a storm is coming. Breaking into a run, I spin around trees and search the dense foliage. He loves to climb, so I'm sure he is up high. *Where are you, Kiwano?*

I hear the raindrops before I feel them. Luckily the umbrella of the jungle protects me from most of the downpour. But as the leaves grow heavy, they will sag and it won't be long before I'll be soaked.

I turn back toward the river and my heart leaps. Huddled high in a *koi* tree, his thin arms clutching his knees, is Kiwano.

"Wee-wee-o." *Clap!* The thunder is closer. The little boy does not move.

"Wee-wee-o! Jaguar!" I cup my hands around my mouth and yell up to him. "Kiwano, come down now! You're the last one; good job!"

He does not hear me.

I try to shake the koi tree, but it doesn't budge. "Kiwano." I hear the panic in my voice and hope he doesn't. "Come down from the tree."

No response.

The rain has reached us, and my hands and feet slip as I climb the smooth trunk of the tree. When I am finally even with the branch where Kiwano is crouched, I touch his arm. "Kiwano, don't be scared. I will get you down."

64

He doesn't move. Peering through the rain, I notice his eyes are clenched and his lips are moving furiously. I lean in.

"Go away, go away, go away," he whispers. "Go away, go away, go away."

"Kiwano, it's Luka. I'm here to take you home. Give me your hand." He does not respond. Bumps rise on my skin. Something is wrong.

I grab him and we half shinny, half fall down the tree.

"Go away, go away, go away," he murmurs in my ear.

He is a small boy, and I run home with him bouncing on my hip like a sack of dried palm fronds. When I get to his hut, I hand him to his maha and turn to get Tukkita.

"What happened?" Before I can take a step, Maha is standing in front of me.

"I don't know. When I found him, he was acting the same way. Maha, what's wrong with him?"

"Nothing," she snaps. "I am sure he just climbed too high and got scared. Go home. Karara fixed dinner."

"No."

Tukkita suddenly appears; I ignore Maha's glare and follow him inside. The shaman leans over the boy and mumbles words I cannot understand. Kiwano is still whispering, "Go away, go away, go away," and the song the two voices make sounds strangely beautiful. Suddenly, Kiwano gasps and sits up. His eyes are wild. Clutching the shaman, the two stare at each other.

"Punhana," he says.

Kiwano's mother falls to the floor wailing. Maha turns gray. I cannot move. The Punhana is the legendary bird of death, the messenger of the Good Gods. As a child, I heard stories about the Punhana, the beautiful bird with an orange and red tail and bright blue wings. It is said to have a crown of feathers the color of a sunset, and a beak as long and green as the *tuta* palm. It always brings its message to a child and it is a simple one: death.

"It is not going to be Kiwano," Tukkita says. "He was just the one who saw the Punhana. Someone else in the village is going to die. Someone important . . ." His voice fades, and he seems to avoid looking in my direction.

"Who?" No one answers me. I turn to the boy, still trembling on the floor. "Kiwano, who did the Punhana say is going to die?"

Kiwano looks at me with cloudy eyes. I lunge for him. "What else did the Punhana say?"

Tukkita shoves me and I fall to the floor, surprised at his strength.

66

"The Punhana does not speak. It only shows itself to two people: the messenger and the person who is going to die. We just have to wait."

"How long? How long do we have to wait?"

"Seven sunsets," my mother murmurs. "The person will die before seven sunsets."

CHAPTER FIVE

TIRIO

12 Years, 360 Days
The United States

"I'm going!" I yell to Sara, bolting out the door.

"Tirio, wait."

"I'll pack when I get home." I shove a water bottle into my backpack and ride my bike out of the garage.

Sara follows me outside, still in her pajamas and holding a bagel. "Where are you off to now?" she asks, taking a bite.

I coast up and give her a kiss on the cheek, catching a whiff of the garlic cream cheese. "The zoo. I promise I'll be back by three."

She pulls back and her eyes light up. "Really? Hold on, I'll go with you. The weather is gorgeous and it's been forever since I've been."

"No!"

She raises an eyebrow in surprise.

"I mean, Joey's already going with me," I quickly continue. "So . . . you probably shouldn't."

"Why?"

"Well . . ." I struggle for an excuse. I don't want her to know that the real reason we're going to the zoo is to train for my test. "He said he had to tell me something. About his dad. So he just might feel funny talking about it in front of you, that's all."

She takes another bite of her bagel and chews on it for a while before nodding in agreement.

"You're right," she says. "You guys should probably spend some time together before we leave."

A wave of guilt washes over me. She believed me so easily.

"Have fun," Sara says, turning toward the house. "Say hi to the clouded leopard for me."

I hop back on my bike and give her one last wave. She lifts her bagel in response and watches me take off. Sara's cool for a mom—and I wish I could tell her the truth—but as laid-back as she is about some stuff, I can't risk her trying to stop me.

Shifting the gears as low as they'll go, I jam down hard into the clips. Like a horse being spurred by a cowboy, the bike powers up the hill. I stand and pedal away from the house. My entire body screams into action—

legs, lungs, heart, feet. I duck my chin to my chest and close my eyes, focusing on how my body is feeling: strong. *I can do it.* Two days alone in the jungle. My skills from the Amazon are coming back to me. My foot's as good as it's ever going to be.

But a little voice keeps taunting me: *Who do you think you are? Your paho decided seven years ago you weren't strong enough to be a Takunami. Why do you think you are now?*

Clenching my jaw, I open my eyes and pedal harder uphill, as if showing my doubts exactly who I am. I reach the crest of the hill and, without even stopping, crouch back, hover over the bike seat, and speed toward the bottom. The doubts chase me. *Are you crazy? You haven't been in the jungle forever. Who are you kidding?* I squint my eyes against the stinging wind and pedal faster. The passing houses become a solid blur, yet one tiny doubt still manages to keep up.

I fishtail around the corner toward Joey's house and skid to a stop in front of the Carters' garage. Throwing my bike down, I race up the porch steps and pound on the door. Joey yells for me to come in. Gasping for breath, I shut the door behind me, slide my back down the wall, and collapse on the floor. The question slips in through the open window and rests in my lap. *What if I die?*

* * *

Miami has a huge wildlife park where the animals roam freely; predator and prey are separated only by moats. After Joey agreed yesterday to help me prepare for this trip, my first thought had been the park.

"The best thing to do," I say as we now hop onto the monorail, "is to try to spot as many animals as possible. That's what my maha had me do when I was a kid. I had to find and name birds, mammals, insects, reptiles, amphibians—anything. The goal was to see them before they saw you."

"Ant!" Joey screams, pointing to the ground whizzing by beneath us.

I manage a laugh. I'm a little nervous that I won't be able to do it like I used to.

"Actually, I'll leave the animal spotting up to you." Joey unfolds the zoo map and places it on his lap, smoothing out the creases. "I'm much better at navigating. My dad taught me all about navigation when he used to fly the smaller planes."

I look at the map in his hand, with its neatly outlined borders and its cartoon animals, and realize how totally opposite this is from the wild jungle. "Maybe this was a dumb idea," I say. "I mean, this is how my maha and I used to train, but it's just not the same."

"You'll do great, Tirio." Joey elbows me as the train takes off. "I know you will. If anyone can do it, you can."

I watch him study the map intently. He's so confident right now, so sure of himself—and of me. I imagine what his face is going to look like when his parents tell him about the divorce. It's going to be a total knockout sucker punch. He's going to be shocked.

"Right." I nod, anxious to get started, to prove to both of us that he's right.

We approach the Asian exhibits. "Showtime."

From past experience, I know the first ride of the day is always the one with the most sightings. Even the shy animals are willing to stay out before it gets too hot.

"Malayan sun bear. Anoa. Banteng. Muntjac." I identify the animals.

Joey looks impressed. "How do you know all that?"

"Sara and I used to come here every week," I explain, feeling more confident now. "She thought it would help make me less homesick for the jungle."

I smile and crane my neck as we move on toward the African exhibits. That was strange. I didn't see the clouded leopard.

The clouded leopard has always been my favorite animal at the zoo. Every time Sara and I came, I refused to leave until I'd spotted him. He was one of the hardest

72

ones to see, and if I could catch sight of him, I still felt the Takunami hunter alive in me. Where was he?

At the end of the first half-hour loop, Joey and I crawl over each other to switch sides. Now that I've spotted the animals on the left, it's time to check out the ones on the right. Joey holds up the map he's been using to keep track of the animals I've found. There's a check mark by more than half of them.

"No wonder you always won at hide-and-seek." He snorts. "You had an unfair advantage."

"Don't be a sore loser." I grin. "You were just never a very good hider."

The train takes off and Joey relaxes back into the bench. The lions are now panting with half-closed eyes, and some of the smaller monitor lizards have positioned themselves within misting distance of the waterfall. I spot a family of gray koalas munching leaves in a eucalyptus tree, a huge komodo dragon retreating into his cave, and a Cape hunting dog squeezing into the disappearing shadow of a boulder. I squint my eyes and scan up and down the tall trees—the clouded leopard's favorite spot. I see the bright green of the leaves and the brown of branches, but no sign of any gold and black spotted fur. I do a quick search of the other trees; no luck. An uneasy feeling settles over me.

By the third loop, the visitor line is longer, and I know this will be our last run. "What animals are left?" I ask Joey as the train departs.

He names eight animals, including the clouded leopard.

I quickly explain that I've never left the zoo without seeing that cat and ask Joey to help me look.

"It's awfully hot," Joey says, folding up the map and using it to fan himself. "Maybe he's hiding out inside one of the caves."

I point out a jabiru stork flapping its wings in the top branches of an oak tree and Joey opens his map to check it off.

Shielding my eyes, I twist around until I can't see the Asian exhibits anymore. "I don't like this, Joe," I whisper.

Suddenly a girl behind us screams. "Look! Over in Monkey Meadow!"

Joey and I jerk our heads around.

"Oh my God," Joey whispers. "Is that what you were looking for?"

Yes. The clouded leopard.

Crouched beneath one of the trees, the small, beautiful cat watches the passing train with wary eyes. He doesn't try to hide or run. He just stares. The brown lifeless body of a baby monkey hangs from his jaws.

The apes are screeching in a million different pitches, the conductor yells into her walkie-talkie, and someone's cell phone starts ringing Beethoven's Fifth, but the sounds fade to silence as the clouded leopard and I lock eyes.

Another sign. No—a warning.

Look for danger when you least expect it. You are never safe.

LUKA

12 Years, 361 Sunrises
The Amazon

"You are kidding." I hear Karara scoff. "I will not wear that thing."

"I am *not* kidding, and you *will* wear it," Maha replies.

"Ask someone else."

"No one else wants to help."

"Hmmmmph, are you surprised?"

Smack! I hear a sharp intake of breath from Karara and then silence.

Dropping the wood I'm carrying, I start toward our hut.

"Luka's sense of smell needs to be tested, and we all must help," Maha continues. "You have caused enough trouble. If you want to enjoy life after his test, then you have to make some sacrifices. Skulking around talking to boys and braiding your hair is not doing Luka any good. I don't care *who* or *what* you think you are; you must do

76

your part. Now put this on and meet me outside."

Maha's footsteps approach the door and I rush back to the dropped wood. As I lean over, I hear her hiss, "And don't even *think* about running to your father. This is the last thing he needs."

Crouched down with the wood in my arms, I freeze.

What? *What?* I must have misunderstood. Karara knows who Paho is? How? For how long? Slowly I stand. Sucking in my cheeks, I pick up the rest of the wood and carry it to the pile. The pieces slam against each other with satisfying clunks as I stack them.

"Luka?" My mother's voice sounds surprised. "I thought you were at the river."

"I was, but I decided to bring some wood back—so you'll have it while I'm gone." I head back toward the forest, away from her suspicious eyes.

"Leave it," she says. "The girls can do it later. It is time for your scent test."

I take a deep breath and turn.

My mother, with eyes like the high-flying *muwipa*, watches me as I approach. I smile, and she seems satisfied that I didn't hear anything. "Sulali!" she yells.

Sulali comes bounding out of the woods, hooting like a monkey and dancing around.

Tambo cowers beside me and eyes Sulali. She has two

squirrel monkey skins wrapped around her neck, and a black-tipped tail peeks out of the back of her dress. One dead monkey is draped over her head, its mouth open in an eternal scream as the teeth anchor in her hair.

I shake my head. "Maha, I don't think this is such a good idea after what happened yesterday."

She ignores me. "Karara."

My older sister, her ponytail divided into eight separate braids, saunters out of our hut holding some capybara skins. A red welt the shape of a hand is rising on her cheek. The mark of a traitor.

Refusing to look at us, she stands by the door, head held high.

"Put them on," my mother orders.

"Later." Karara's voice does not waver, but when Sulali races over to take her hand, Karara clutches it.

Neither woman speaks, and I am enjoying the silent battle until finally my mother continues. "In the past few days, Luka, we have tested your taste, hearing, and sight. Today, we will test your sense of smell. Sulali and Karara will be hiding in the forest. Your goal is to find them."

"Maha, after everything that happened yesterday with the Punhana, I really don't want to do this." She starts walking toward me. "Maybe if we—"

Opening her hand, she throws something in my face.

"Aaaarghhhh." I claw at my burning eyes.

"Do not worry," she says. "The effects of the potion will only last for the rest of the morning; then your sight will return. Your vision will be blurry, but you will still be able to see shapes and movement. This is to ensure you only use your nose to find the girls."

Tears flood my eyes, trying to put out the fire burning them.

"Karara?" Sulali whimpers.

"He's fine," Karara says. "Let's go."

Sulali's hand brushes against my leg as my sisters head toward the woods. I feel Tambo creep away from beside me.

"Tambo, stay!" Maha orders.

Fighting my body's natural instinct, I open my eyes and see the faint outline of my mother.

"This could easily happen in the forest," Maha says. "A sting from a *ruyana* wasp, a bite from a *pino* viper. You need to know how to get around without your eyesight. Follow the path until you reach the garden; begin looking there. I collected urine from the animals the hunters brought back yesterday and scattered a trail from both the squirrel monkey and the capybara. The smell should lead you to where each girl is hiding. When you have found them, call out their names and they will answer you. You must make your way home by yourself before the potion wears off."

"Maha, please don't make me do this." I wipe the tears from my eyes.

She is silent and I begin to feel hopeful, but when she speaks her voice is strangely quiet. "Time is running out, Luka. Now go."

Using my fingers to hold open my reluctant eyes, I focus on the ground and stumble toward the garden.

Time is running out. There was something in the way my mother said it, something I had never heard before.

Fear.

I stop. Maha is never scared—ever. I jump sideways as something skitters past me on the trail.

Sinking to the ground, I feel my heart beginning to thud. She knows who is going to die. That is why she threw the potion into my eyes. Not so I couldn't see my sisters, but so I couldn't see the Punhana.

It is me. *My* time is running out. *I* am the one who's going to die within a week.

As I sit there wondering what my family's done to deserve this, my fear gradually turns to anger.

It's Karara's fault. She has angered the forest spirits by finding out who our father is. Because of her curiosity, her stupid pride and bitterness, she has brought this bad luck to our family. It doesn't take a shaman to figure out that I am going to be sacrificed as revenge for my sister's act. I wipe my cheeks. Although most of the stinging is gone, my eyes continue to flood.

Karara knows her place in the tribe, but apparently she's above the rules. That's why she doesn't cut her hair, so she'll stand out from all the other girls. She thinks she's smarter and stronger than me because she knows our paho. Well, we'll see about that. *We'll see just how strong you are, sister.*

Widening my eyes, I stand and march toward the garden, unconcerned about being bitten by anything poisonous. The only spider I have to worry about has eight braids instead of eight legs.

The smell of fresh soil greets me at the garden and I immediately pick up the scent of the two urine trails, one a little sweeter and the other more acidic.

Following the sweeter one, I head off to find my monkey sister. Maha wound the trail in circles that backtrack across each other, attempting to make the test difficult. The path is farther than I thought, and twice I step on something that hisses in protest. Another time, a low-hanging vine pokes me in the eye and when I jerk back, my head cracks against a tree.

Clenching my fists, I growl and continue the hunt.

A few steps later, the urine trail ends, and I peer up into the branches of the *chukka* palm—a favorite of the squirrel monkey.

"Sulali?" I see the blurred movement of a body sliding down the tree, and a giggling Sulali hugs my knees.

"Good job, Luka. Am I the first one?" She grabs my hand and leads me back to the path. "Do your eyes hurt? I'm glad you didn't take too long. I was trying to be very quiet and not move, but these skins are very itchy and—"

"Sulali, you must go home now," I interrupt. "I still have to find Karara. Follow the path back to the hut and wait for me there."

"Why don't I just wait for you here in the garden? I don't mind. Tambo followed you anyway; he can keep me company. Please, Luka. I won't cause any trouble, I promise. *Pleeeease.*"

"Just by staying here you will be causing trouble. You heard what Maha said; you must go back. Plus, I want her to know how quickly I found you," I lie. "So run. You and Tambo race back and tell Maha how well I did."

"Ooooh, you're right. That will cheer her up. I will run as fast as I can. C'mon, Tambo, you fatty, let's go!" she shrieks, and takes off.

I close my eyes and listen to her footsteps fade. A

toucan flaps overhead and calls to its mate. A twig snaps to my left and my eyes flash open. I squint toward the sound, but see nothing and back away. I walk until I reach the coolness of shade, and with outreached hands I find the tree it belongs to. Sliding my back against the trunk, I sit and wait. The sun moves one foot length. Then two. My vision is returning and I know it's time to head home. Walking past the bitter urine trail of the capybara, I enter the clearing of the garden and turn in a circle, waving. *Good-bye, sister. Good-bye.*

I have no trouble finding my way back to the hut, and when Maha asks me where Karara is, I raise my eyebrows in surprise. "What? I found her soon after I found Sulali. She should have returned a long time ago."

"It's almost dark. Where is she?" My mother purses her lips and narrows her eyes. "This is her way of getting out of chores. I told you she was lazy."

Maha seizes a torch and storms into the forest. I tiptoe after her, amazed how easy it is to function in the dark after having imperfect vision. Finally Karara will get what she deserves.

Upon reaching the garden, Maha lifts the torch and peers back. I dart behind a tree. Finally, she shines the light into the forest in front of her. "Karara," she whispers, narrowing her eyes. "Where are you? Get out here."

I hear the rustling of leaves as my oldest sister steps into the glow of the light and throws the capybara skins at Maha's feet. "I guess your wonderful son is not as ready as you thought."

"What are you talking about? He said he found you hours ago."

"Ha. Not even close." Karara smirks.

"Quiet!" Maha grabs Karara's arm. "Do you want everyone to hear you? I told you to come home after Luka found you."

"And *I* told *you*, Luka never found me." Karara rips her arm away and spins back toward the village. *Whap!* Karara's braids slap Maha across the face.

Grabbing the knife on her belt, Maha seizes Karara by the hair. In the light of the falling torch, I watch my sister jerk back and yelp. The knife glints as it slices through the air, and I hear Karara scream.

My heart drums so loudly against my ribs, I'm sure Maha hears it. The dropped torch struggles to stay lit, but the dampness of the forest floor sucks at it hungrily. Suddenly, it dances into the sky and flares to life. In the ring of light Maha sneers down at a form beneath her and lifts something up triumphantly. I ram my fist into my mouth.

"This is your fault, my daughter. You are always causing problems. From the day you came out as a girl and not a boy, you have been a burden. You are a Takunami. It is time you start acting—and looking—like one." She holds up what I now recognize as Karara's black ponytail of braids. "When you are ready to accept that, you are welcome back into my home."

Maha strides away, but pauses by where I am hiding and illuminates me with the torchlight. "Luka, *mmpah*! Let's go!"

"But . . ."

"*Now.*"

I step onto the path and turn toward my sister.

Maha grabs me. "Luka, *now*!"

As we walk away, Karara sobs into the earth, and overhead I hear the flapping of a large bird. My mouth goes dry.

The Punhana.

CHAPTER SIX

TIRIO

12 Years, 361–362 Days

Joey shows up at our house half an hour before Sara and I are to leave for the airport.

"Just came to say good-bye," he says, watching me throw my backpack into the Jeep. He lowers his voice. "And to wish you luck. Have you figured out a plan yet?"

"Sneaking out shouldn't be too hard, since I should have my own room. And I'm definitely leaving at night. No matter how much harder it's going to be in the dark, I need as much of a head start as possible before they begin looking for me. Besides, it'll be easier to take one of the camp canoes then."

"Do you remember how to get back to your village?" he asks anxiously. "Will you be able to find your tributary?"

"Well, it's not like I can MapQuest it or anything,

86

and honestly, that's the part I'm most nervous about . . .
the navigation. I can handle the survival part, but knowing which way to go without getting help from my
father . . ." I shake my head. "I'm hoping to use a combination of things looking familiar, my senses, and, as
crazy as it might sound to you, the spirit world looking
after me."

Joey shrugs. "Considering that Sara found you floating in a tiny boat on the world's largest river, I'd say someone is looking out for you . . . spirit world, Lady Luck,
fate."

Leaning against the car door, I decide to change the
subject. "So you guys are still going to dinner tonight,
huh?"

"What? To Las Conchitas?" He nods. "Of course."

For once I wish his dad *had* cancelled. Bad weather,
stuck landing gear, dog got loose on the runway . . . anything. The thought must show on my face, because Joey
punches my shoulder and says, "Don't worry, I'll order
the Las Conchitas combination platter number three in
your honor."

"Gee, thanks."

He rolls his eyes dramatically. "What are friends for?"

What are friends for? *Friends are for being honest
about what's really going to happen tonight,* I think. *Friends*

87

are for warning you that your parents are going to drop a bomb on you. He'd never believe you, I remind myself.

"You nervous?" he asks quietly.

"Not yet," I admit. "Strangely enough."

The front door slams and we both turn and watch Sara lock up. Joey picks up the bike he's left lying in the driveway and wheels it toward me. "Good luck, man. Be careful," he says.

"I will," I say. "You too."

Joey raises an eyebrow and then shakes his head. "You'll do great, T. I mean it. You will."

"Thanks."

The bright orange ball of sun drops into the horizon in front of us as we approach the airport. I stare out the window at the palm trees lined up like soldiers at the entrance of Miami International. My eyes search the fronds for things that might be hiding, but I know I won't find anything. No deadly snakes or poisonous spiders, no hungry cats ready to pounce. It suddenly dawns on me how safe my life has been since I arrived here.

I shudder as I recall the staring eyes of the dead baby monkey yesterday. Even in broad daylight, he hadn't seen his killer sneaking up on him. He felt safe. Was that a warning from the Good Gods? Were they telling me to stay away? Like the poison of a curare-tipped arrow, this doubt spreads through my body, and suddenly I find it difficult to breathe.

We park the car and I strap on my backpack. Straightening my shoulders, I welcome the noises that surround me as we walk into the terminal: the clicking of a Seeing Eye dog's nails, the zipping of a suitcase, the polite sneeze of an elderly woman. All the way to the gate and even after we've boarded, I focus on identifying and locating sounds. With each one, I feel more in control.

"Okay, let's go over the itinerary again," Sara says after we've been in the air for about an hour. "We'll fly directly into São Paulo, Brazil, and then on to Manaus, where Juan Diego will meet us and transport us to the research camp. Each morning I want to visit one of the tribes I'm following up with." She grabs my arm and squeezes it. "It's going to be a blast, Tirio." Her face glows as she describes each of the four tribes. "I bet the Ipinipos can teach you that tribal dance you wanted to learn. And the Qwetinatu are great climbers—for your kapok." Typical Sara, she doesn't push anymore than that, just drops the hint and then goes on explaining how we're going to spend the rest of the time.

I watch the excitement in her movements as she continues to speak and realize how easy it would be to just hang out with her all day and forget the test. It would be so easy.

But as I watch a boy and his father play cards in the row next to us, I know I can't. This opportunity won't come to me again.

The video being shown on the televisions is a *National Geographic* special on the Amazonian rain forest, and my eyes keep searching for monkeys and birds hidden in the trees. The honeymooning couple two rows behind us whisper and giggle until my ears almost twist backward listening to what they're saying. One of the flight attendants is wearing a jasmine perfume and every time she's near, my nose goes into overdrive.

Feeling the weight of a blanket, I look up to see Sara reaching for something in the overhead bin. She pulls out a couple of overstuffed miniature white pillows and hands one to me.

"I'm going to try to get some sleep," she murmurs as she plops back down. "We're going to be there before you know it, and I want to hit the ground running."

Hit the ground running. I'm amazed by her choice of words.

The cabin lights dim, the in-flight movie begins, and the newlyweds behind me finally quiet. I stare out the window. The blackness of the sky transforms the plastic into a mirror, and I trace the outline of my nose, my eyes, my ears, my mouth. I remember my maha's last words: *If only your body was as strong as your spirit.* "It is, Maha," I whisper to the face looking back at me. "It is."

Leaning my head against the pillow, I focus on the humming drone of the engines and finally feel myself falling asleep.

"Tirio, we're here." Sara's shaking me, and I wake to see the passengers around me standing and stretching.

We're here? I bolt up and crack my head on the overhead bin.

Sara winces. "Ouch."

I wrestle my backpack from underneath my seat and smash my leg into the armrest as I hurry to stand behind her.

"It's gonna be a while, Tirio," Sara says, raising an eyebrow and gesturing toward the long line of people in front of us.

"Right," I say, rubbing my head where I hit it. No need to rush.

Immigration is no problem, and we quickly board a smaller plane for our second leg. We've barely finished drinking our complimentary passion fruit drink before the pilot informs us we will soon be landing in the city of Manaus.

A grinning, freshly showered Juan Diego is waiting for us outside the airport. He looks exactly like I remember him, except perhaps a little rounder. He gives Sara a long hug before finally turning to me and offering his hand. "I don't think we've met," he teases.

"Tirio," I say, playing along.

"No!" His mouth drops in pretend shock. "You are not Tirio. Tirio is a small boy about this tall." He measures to his waist. "With thin arms, puny little legs, and a voice like a girl."

Sara laughs. "Them's fightin' words, Juan Diego."

"Well, I certainly wouldn't want to get in a fight with this young man," Juan Diego says, looking me up and down. "No doubt I'd lose."

I stand up straighter and they both laugh.

"Man, oh man." Juan Diego shakes his head as we walk toward the baggage claim. "Unbelievable."

Have I really changed that much? My heart swells.

After a half-hour ride with a chattering Juan Diego, I'm finally standing back on the bank of the Amazon. I stare out at the massive brown river. It hasn't changed at all.

92

The water in the cove where we're docked is calm as glass, but a stone's toss away, the current churns and sucks at branches and logs, eyeing our boat greedily. Kneeling, I dig my hands into the mud and breathe in the earthy odor. I shiver. From the water, the ground, and every tree limb, I feel a thousand eyes watching me. The jungle knows I'm back. The question is, will it let me in?

Juan Diego unloads the supplies from town into the boat, and the mud groans in protest as he pushes the boat away from the shore.

"Tirio, I would love to give you some time to reminisce, but we've got to go if we want to get to camp before dusk," he says.

"Right." I climb in and sit next to Sara.

"We've come a long way since the last time we were here, huh?" she says, putting her arm around my shoulders and scooting toward me.

I nod.

The roar of the boat engine makes it impossible to speak, so Sara and I just sit in silence for the next four hours—reconnecting with the Amazon in our own ways. I spot flashes of tail feathers in the trees, I listen to the many species of frogs debate the abundance of flies this year, and my stomach growls at the smells of meat cooking in the villages we zoom past. By the time we pull into the research center, my head is buzzing like a swarm of a million bees, but when I see the thatched huts of the research camp, everything quiets.

"Here we are," Juan Diego says, docking the boat. "Just in time for dinner." He steps out and offers Sara his hand. "Let's eat first, and then we'll get you guys settled."

I leap onto the shore and spin around. "It feels like we never left, doesn't it?"

Sara scans the area as she considers my question. "You're right, T. Things haven't really changed much in seven years, have they?"

"Well, fortunately for us, the cooking has changed . . . it's gotten better," Juan Diego says, patting his protruding belly. "And if we don't get up there soon, there will be nothing left."

"But what about our bags?" Sara asks.

"I'll send someone down for them." He starts up the hill. "Since we started housing tour groups, we have people to do that now."

Sara raises her eyebrows at me. "I guess some things have changed."

After a delicious meal in which I have two helpings, knowing it will be my last real food for a while, Juan Diego offers to show us to our hut.

We enter the last hut in the compound, and my heart skips a beat when I see both our suitcases inside.

"Since there's no electricity," Juan Diego reminds us, "you'll have to use candles for light." He opens a dresser drawer by the bed and pulls out a box of matches, checking to see how many are left. "Sorry about not being able to give you each your own room," he says, closing the drawer. "We'd normally have space, but it just so happens we're full this week." He shrugs. "I guess everyone wants to see the rain forest before it is completely destroyed."

"Wait a minute," I say, panic rising in my throat. How am I going to sneak out with Sara sleeping two feet away from me? "Sara and I are staying in the same room?"

Sara unzips the front pocket of her purse and pulls out a couple of halogen headlamps. "What are you complaining about, T?" she asks, handing me one and putting on the other. "You're the one who snores like an eighty-year-old grandpa with a deviated septum."

She winks at me and Juan Diego laughs, heading for the door. "I'm sure you both are tired," he says. "So I'll let you unpack while you enjoy tonight's musical entertainment, provided by the camp's very own jungle orchestra and led by our resident howler monkey, Kimbo."

"I can't imagine any sweeter music," Sara says, smiling.

After Juan Diego leaves, I frantically scan the room

for a backup escape route. The area is much smaller than I remember, and since Sara's already claimed the bed by the door, that's out. The only other exit is through a window. There are two of them, one to the left of the door and the other above my bed. I walk over and run my fingers over the mesh. It's thin enough to cut, and I am thankful that Juan Diego gave us an end unit. Relieved that my plan is back on track, I turn around and unzip my suitcase.

The room is quickly getting darker as the sun sets, and I reach up to twist on my headlamp. A huge roach, disturbed by the light, scuttles from under the nightstand between Sara and me.

"Megaloblatta blaberoides."

"Mwe-cota."

We blurt out the names at the same time—Sara giving the scientific; me, the Takunami.

"Is that what your tribe called them?" She laughs. *"Mwe-cota?"*

"Yeah," I say, shocked at how the name had just popped into my head.

"That's pretty amazing that you remember such an obscure word after all these years," she says as she shoves her suitcase under the bed. "I mean—*food, water, sky, river*—those words I understand you being able to recall, but . . . *roach*?" She stands and dusts off her hands. "Wow . . ."

"Yeah, I'm surprised too," I say, ducking my chin to avoid blinding her with my light. How did that just happen? Are things truly coming back to me like I'd hoped, or is someone else helping me? And if so . . . who?

Disappearing into the darkness of the bathroom to put away my toothbrush, I see something skitter across the floorboards and shine my headlamp toward it. A thin gray tail disappears into a hole behind the toilet— a *sumiha*—the name of a mouse rests on my tongue. Unbelievable. I smile in the darkness. Not that knowing the name of a roach or a mouse is going to help me with my *soche seche tente*, but these sudden shots of memory give me the confidence that anything is possible.

When I return to the other room, it's empty and I find Sara outside on the porch.

"The perfect Amazon evening," she says, leaning over the railing.

The banging of pots from the camp kitchen harmonizes with the chirping of the crickets as we settle into the bamboo chairs on the porch. Like a show-stealing tenor, a howler monkey interrupts by huffing out a territorial warning.

"Just as Juan Diego promised," I say.

We sit a little longer in silence until finally Sara starts talking. "There's something I need to discuss with you, Tirio."

Her voice sounds serious and my heart speeds up. "Okay."

"I was in your room yesterday, and I found something that you probably didn't want me to see." She turns toward me, and the beam of her headlamp shines directly into my face.

I look down, not only to shield my eyes but also to hide my shock at what she just said. The letter. Oh my God, she found the letter I'd left in my backpack.

"I'm not even going to pretend to understand why you'd do this," she continues. "Not only is it stupid, but it's dangerous and you could really hurt yourself." She's still looking in my direction, and with the light beamed on me, I feel like a prisoner being interrogated.

"You don't understand, Sara," I say quietly. "I have to do this."

The howler monkey begins again, and it sounds like a jet engine taking off.

"Why?" She raises her voice, and I'm not sure if it's because she's angry or whether it's to be heard over him. Either way, she sounds mad. "To prove how tough you are? How macho? That's just stupid, Tirio. I mean, honestly." She finally looks away, and her beam lights up the makeshift soccer goal in the center yard.

Stupid? I feel the anger well up inside me. How dare she say that? "You have no idea what it's like to be me," I say.

"You're right," she agrees calmly. "I don't know what it's like to have a physical handicap. But I'll tell you one thing—if I did, and I worked as hard as you have to overcome it, I certainly wouldn't risk reinjuring myself by hiding the only thing that's keeping me healthy in an old pair of sneakers in my closet."

The howler quiets, and I imagine his expression being as shocked as mine.

"What?" I ask.

"I found your orthotic in an old pair of cleats, Tirio." She sighs. "Stuffed under two other boxes in your closet and looking like it hadn't been worn for quite a while— I'm just going to take a wild guess and say . . . since you took them off last season."

I let out a short laugh and bury my head in my hands in relief. My orthotic. She hadn't been talking about the letter, she'd been talking about my orthotic. I keep chuckling.

"I'm glad you can find the humor in the situation, Tirio," Sara says. "Because I don't."

"No, no, you're right," I agree, trying not to smile. "It's not funny at all. I just . . . I just . . ." I pause, not knowing how to continue. "I just can't imagine how bad those old cleats must have smelled when you took the lid off that box. I thought for sure that would be the perfect hiding place."

Sara gives a small smile, and I know she's not really mad. "It was pretty noxious, I'll admit. Why aren't you wearing it, Tirio?"

"I'm trying to wean myself, Sara," I answer truthfully. "I don't want to have to wear it for the rest of my life."

"Why not? No one can see it. No one knows."

I shrug. "I just want to be normal like everyone else."

She puts her hand on my shoulder. "You're never going to be just like everyone else, Tirio," she says. "And that's a good thing. Believe me. Being normal is boring. And if there's one thing you aren't, it's boring."

Sara holds out my orthotic. "Promise me you'll wear this from here on out," she says.

I take it and nod. *As soon as I'm finished with my soche seche tente, I will, Sara,* I think. *I promise.*

"I have a bad feeling you'll regret it if you don't."

"Okay."

She stands. "I think we should go to bed. We've got a

big day ahead of us tomorrow. You ready?"

The jungle chatters around me, the Takunami names quickly replacing the American ones. The potoo becomes a *qui-ra*; a bay owl, a *kwanho*; the blue-tailed bee-eater, a *tsu-fle*.

I stare out into the darkness of the rain forest for a second, repeating her question in my mind. "Yes," I say, getting up. "I *am* ready."

LUKA

12 Years, 362 Sunrises
The Amazon

Maha shakes me. "Get up."

"Where's Karara?" I turn to look at her hammock. Empty. I couldn't fall asleep after we got home because I kept thinking about my sister in the jungle. Every noise I heard, I was sure was her, but I must have dozed off when she didn't come back by daybreak. "Is she outside?"

"She is not home." My mother sweeps the floor. "She will be back when she gets hungry enough. Karara is a stubborn girl, but pride doesn't feed an empty stomach. Here, eat this, and then we will complete your last preparation test." She hands me some dried fish and manioc bread.

"Maha, I think we should look for her. I'm worried she might be hurt or . . ." I look away, afraid to say my biggest fear.

"Don't be foolish. Eat your breakfast. I want to finish the test early so you have time to rest before seeing Tukkita this afternoon."

I'd forgotten about my meeting with the shaman. Every boy must receive a blessing before the night of his soche seche tente—in case he doesn't come back. No matter how much a boy has prepared or how strong he is, evil spirits planted by enemy tribes will take a boy down just as easily as a jaguar.

"I heard a bird last night as we were leaving Karara," I mumble with a mouthful of manioc. "What if it was the Punhana?"

Maha shoots me a look of disgust. "It is *your* life we are worried about, not your sister's. I am going to the river to wash. Wait for me here."

I watch her leave and count to thirty. Peeking out the front door to make sure no one is around, I sprint past the men's rohacas and down the path toward the garden. I have to find my sister.

"Luka." Behind me, my mother spits out my name like a bite of bad papaya. "Where are you going?"

I stop and turn. Maha is standing in the middle of the trail with one hand digging into her cocked hip and a woven basket in the other.

"I only hope you can follow directions from your father better than you do from me," she says, walking up and placing the basket on the ground.

"I just . . ."

Untying her leather belt, she steps toward me. "Since you don't want to enjoy your morning meal, we'll begin your test now. You'll wear a blindfold for this one."

The nagging feeling about the Punhana returns. Once more, I am being prevented from seeing.

"Today's test will rely on your sense of touch." She tugs the leather evenly over my eyes. "You will be doing things with your hands only, things you may have to do in the dark, whether it is the darkness of the jungle or the darkness caused by blindness." We walk farther down the trail. "Six steps in front of you there is a *kana-puta* tree. Climb it."

Stretching out my arms, I take six steps and touch the smooth bark of a *stana-kila*. Wrong tree! I jerk my hands back, but it's too late. A swarm of ants races onto my bare skin, and within seconds I feel like I have been thrown into a thornbush. I dance around, pounding and rubbing them off, but like the tiny soldiers they are, they don't give up. They have a buddy system with the stana-kila tree. They live in its trunk, drinking the sweet water it produces and, in return, they protect the tree from intruders—in

104

this case, me. I fling off the last clinging ant. "Maha!"

"That was my fault; I pointed you in the wrong direction. Lesson learned: now you know what a stana-kila tree *feels* like as well as what it looks like." She spins me around. "Just stretch out your arm and now you will feel the kana-puta. Climb."

"Maha?"

"I'm not lying this time, Luka," she reassures me. "Climb."

I reach for the tree and jab it with my finger. It *is* a kana-puta this time. Hugging the smooth trunk with my arms and legs, I turn my feet outward and begin to climb. My big toe automatically pulls away from the rest of the foot as it clings to the bark.

"You are going too slowly, Luka. What if there was a peccary charging you? You have thirty counts. One, two, three . . ."

I push off with my legs and reach my arms up again.

"Six, seven, eight . . ."

I anchor myself and feel my way up the cool bark.

"Ten, eleven, twelve . . ."

"How high do I have to go?"

"Thirteen, fourteen, fifteen . . . I will tell you when to stop. Faster!"

The branches of the kana-puta don't start until pretty high up, but I don't know how tall this tree is. "Am I near the top?"

"Eighteen, nineteen, twenty. You have ten body lengths to go. There you will feel a branch with a bunch of plantains hanging from it. Grab them and start down."

I pause. Plantains? In a kana-puta? Is this another trick?

"I put them there," she answers my unasked question. "Twenty-three, twenty-four, twenty-five . . ."

I speed up my shinny. Push, reach, push, reach. I grope above me for the branch—nothing.

"Twenty-nine, thirty. *Thirty*, Luka . . . *thirty*."

Springing off my anchored feet, I feel my head crack as it bangs against a branch.

"Get the plantains."

Grappling with the knot, I untie the fruit, hold the stem in my mouth, and carefully lower myself to the ground.

"Next time you must be faster," Maha scolds.

I rub my scalp. "Can I take the blindfold off now?"

"No, I will lead you to the next part of the test." Maha grabs my hand. Jerking me forward, Maha seems to speed up rather than slow down and gives an angry snort every time I stumble. Finally she stops. "Sit. In the jun-

106

gle, you will need to sleep somewhere off the ground. In front of you are fronds from the wah-pu. Weave a hammock. Go."

I gingerly reach forward, expecting something to bite me. Maha laughs.

I have been weaving since I could walk, so this should not be difficult, but it will take some time to weave a whole hammock. I arrange ten fronds side by side and begin overlapping them, every once in a while checking for holes. The *swish, swish, swish* of the brushing leaves lulls me into my thoughts.

Over, under, over, under.

Just like Karara braiding her hair.

Over, under, over, under.

She won't be doing that anymore.

Over, under, over, under.

Will she grow it long again?

Over, under, over, under.

Will Maha cut Sulali's hair?

Over, under, feel for holes.

Is Karara back?

Over, under, over, under.

What if she dies?

Over, under, over, under.

The spirits will be angry.

Over, under, over, under.

They probably already are.

Over, under, over, under.

They'll never let me complete my soche seche tente.

Stop.

Maybe I don't deserve to.

"Luka?" my mother asks.

"Maha, I think you can see I know what I'm doing. Do I really need to finish?"

She is silent. "You are right. It is almost noon and you still have one more test. The last part is perhaps the most dangerous, but I won't let anything bad happen to you."

I stand and she grabs my elbow. We walk for a while until she shoves a narrow vine into my hand.

"Fifteen steps in front of us is the den of an agouti," Maha whispers. "Except an agouti is not living there; a *wa-chu-chu* spider is."

I take a step back, but she yanks me forward.

"Silly boy, I told you I would not let anything happen to you," she hisses. "My future is also at stake here. Why would I be so stupid?"

"Maha, the bite from a wa-chu-chu is deadly."

"You will not get bitten." Her nails dig into my arm as she tightens her grip.

I step back again. "We have enough food; it is not necessary to kill one. Doing so will anger the Good Gods."

"We are not going to kill it. You are just going to lure it out." She stands behind me and with all her weight pushes me.

I stumble forward. "There has to be another way."

"Stop talking and listen. If you get bitten, it will be your own fault," she says. "As you know, the *ku-stuh* wasp lures the spider out by walking over its web. That is all you are going to do, lure it out. Once I see the spider fully, we will let it know who we are; it will retreat and we will leave."

I have seen a wa-chu-chu devour a fer-de-lance by sucking it dry until there was nothing left but skin. I shudder in the midday heat.

"Now kneel, and I will guide the vine to the lair," she murmurs. "The rest is up to you."

I lower myself, and she directs my hand. At first I don't move. Takunami boys are taught to lure wa-chu-chus out of their lairs from a very young age, but it feels wrong attempting it without all five senses. Maha flicks my ear as a signal to begin.

I lift the vine off the ground and skip it across the silky web. I skip it back, my actions becoming those of a struggling insect. Two more times across, and Maha pokes me. She sees it. I do too. I have done this so many times, even blindfolded I can visualize the spider peeking out.

Skip, skip, skip.

It cautiously creeps forward.

Skip, skip, skip.

A hairy leg probes for the intruder.

Skip, skip, skip.

Not easily fooled. The spider scurries back inside.

I begin again.

Skip, skip, skip.

Feeling threatened, it hisses and shoots out tiny hairs from its body. I jerk away.

Skip, skip, skip.

The vibrations are too much of a temptation. The hungry spider sneaks out again.

Skip, skip. My "insect" is getting tired as I pretend to be caught in the web.

I feel weight on the vine and Maha yells. The spider jumps off and scuttles away deep below us.

"Very good." Maha takes off the blindfold. "Don't you feel silly now for making such a fuss? *Mmpah*— let's go."

I grin and stand. I didn't really think I could do it.

And now Maha is letting me walk home without the blindfold. Things are starting to look up. The birds sing around me and the howlers hoot their approval. The jungle is happy for me.

I follow Maha home, every once in a while closing my eyes to test myself some more. My stomach growls and my throat is dry, but I smile and wave the vine around like Sulali. I *am* ready.

As we enter the village, Tukkita pulls my mother aside and whispers something into her ear.

I chuckle. He is probably telling her where they are going to take me tonight.

My mother's eyes widen, roll back into her head, and she collapses.

"Maha!" I rush over. "Tukkita, what happened?"

"Not here," he says.

We carry Maha to our hut and lay her down in her hammock. "It's Karara, isn't it?"

Tukkita stares out the open door with faraway, bloodshot eyes. He has been talking to the spirit world.

"Tukkita—please," I plead with him.

"Someone has seen the Punhana," he says.

My stomach drops. "Karara?"

"No, although she was there." He sways back and forth.

"Who? Sulali? No, not Sulali!" I spin around, looking

111

for my younger sister.

"It was not Sulali." Unable to stand any longer, Tukkita sinks onto the hammock next to Maha.

"Who?"

"Your paho."

"What?"

"At midday, your father saw the Punhana."

Paho? What about my soche seche tente? Guilt washes over me. I just lost my father, and I am worried about a test? *I can't do it without him. He has to live at least three more days.*

"How long does he have?"

"He is already gone, Luka." The shaman searches the rafters, as though watching the spirit of my father float above us. "Soon after he saw the bird, your paho died."

CHAPTER SEVEN

TIRIO

12 Years, 363 Days
The Amazon

While I lay in my bed, waiting for Sara to fall asleep, I made a deal with the Good Gods: if they wanted me to leave tonight, they would send me a sign. Now, as I cut open the screen with my nail clippers and climb out of our room, a full moon shines down on me—one of the most powerful spirits of all.

The Takunami believe it's impossible to separate the physical and spiritual worlds so, when I was younger, I used signs to make decisions a lot. After a couple of years living in Florida, I stopped looking for them. Now that I've returned, it doesn't feel strange to search for these signs again.

The night animals serenade me, and their Takunami names pop into my head. An invisible hand pulls me toward the river and, after replacing the screen as best as

I can, I head down the path.

Throwing my backpack into the outboard canoe, I untie the boat and push it from the shore. It's heavier than I thought, and I'm thankful the water is high. The current yanks at it eagerly and I barely manage to haul myself into the boat before the river whisks it downstream.

A flock of nesting birds squawks and fills the sky around me. Worried that someone will hear, I hold my breath as I drift away from the research camp and count the seconds until I can start the motor. Joey's dad had a boat we used to take out at night to gig flounder, so I know I won't have any problem cranking this one over, but it seems an eternity until I feel safe enough to even try.

The moon provides plenty of light for me to dodge floating logs, but when the propeller hits something, I realize I have to watch for submerged objects too. The last thing I want is to get tangled in a vine.

After cruising for an hour or so, I slow down and look for a marker that might signal which direction to go. There are over a thousand tributaries; my tribe's village might be down any one of them.

The Amazon is so wide that even with a full moon, I can't see both shores unless I make S turns between the banks. I head to the left and peer behind me as the black outline of a smaller river disappears from view. Was that my tributary? I reach to turn the boat around, but instead of gunning the throttle, I accidentally shut it off. Slamming my fist against the motor casing in frustration, I jump up to pull the starter cord.

I flinch as I see something large disappear under the boat. Sinking back onto the wooden seat, I inch away from the side and slide toward the center. Caimans have been known to jump out of the water, snatch people from canoes, and then disappear before the person has time to scream. I scan the surrounding water for any sign of the animal.

Unhooking the canoe's spotlight, I turn it on, and squint as the brightness makes the inside of the boat glow. Once my eyes have adjusted, I rummage through the toolbox for a weapon. Wait a minute; that's it! Since I can't see both sides, I'll cruise along one bank and illuminate the other with the spotlight.

Starting the motor again, I position the throttle to slow and flash the spotlight across the river. It beams over the couple hundred feet of water, brightening the trees. Then I shine it downriver and stop at a pair of orange eyes staring at me. A dwarf caiman.

I'm not really worried about the dwarf and the spectacled caiman; they're pretty harmless. It's their big brother, the black caiman, I have to look out for. During the day, the difference between the reptiles is obvious by their size and color, but in the dark, the only way to tell them apart is by the reflection of their eyes. The spectacled caiman has eyes that shine yellow, the dwarf's shine orange, and the black caiman's shine red.

Behind the first pair, another set of orange eyes pops up, then another . . . and another. Twenty feet to the left, a row of yellow eyes lines up parallel to the orange ones. I have never seen so many caimans, even on TV specials. I speed the boat forward.

What in the world? As far as the beam reaches, there is a blinking line of yellow and orange irises. I idle the motor. It looks like runway lights at an airport.

I turn the spotlight off and then turn it back on again. The eyes haven't moved.

Blinking yellow. Proceed with caution, like at a stoplight.

I guide the boat between the two rows of eyes. As I turn around a bend in the river, I see a tributary on the left. Is it mine? I steer the boat toward it.

Blink, blink. Red eyes. Ruby-red eyes.

I slam the boat into reverse.

Idling, I stare at the black caiman's eyes blocking the tributary.

RED. STOP. DON'T ENTER.

I turn back toward the main river. Blinking yellow eyes pull me forward.

I keep going straight.

After a while the eyes spread out, and I wonder if I made a mistake. What if I passed my river an hour ago? My heart starts beating faster. What if these caiman eyes aren't really a sign from the Good Gods after all?

RED, RED. RED, RED. I kill the motor. The main river in front of me is blocked by two huge black caimans. The irises glowering at me are the size of my fist. Where do I go now? I spotlight both sides of the bank, looking for a smaller river.

Nothing.

I shine on the red eyes. They're still there. Where are my yellow and orange eyes?

I scan the river. Then I see it: the clay lick. One of the last things I remember before Sara rescued me was a blurry wall of color. When I asked Sara about it later, she told me that parrots gnaw at the clay to neutralize the poison from the fruit they eat. The colors I had seen were a flock of birds. Although the rock barely peeks above the water, I have a feeling this is my clay lick . . . my tributary.

I spin the boat toward it and almost cheer when I turn the corner and see four pairs of yellow eyes beckoning me in. The small river snakes sharply around the wall and then disappears. I would have missed this if not for the caiman roadblock.

Scanning the river behind me, I look for the red eyes. They are gone. So are the yellow and orange ones. Even if they are dangerous, caimans are the pets of the Good Gods—raised and released for the use of my tribe—and I am thankful.

As the sky ahead of me begins to lighten, I continue up the tributary. Realizing I'm slouched over, I straighten up in my seat and stretch. I made it! I sneaked out of the camp, recognized the animal signs, and the Good Gods are apparently helping me. Three great things. I find myself grinning. For the first time since I decided to take the test, I feel like there's a very good chance that I'm going to succeed. I really might make it back!

I don't know where or when I'm going to stop, but I'm sure there will be another sign. I just have to recognize it. As soon as the thought enters my brain, the boat engine begins to sputter. The gas. I could transfer the hose to the second gas tank and continue, but, as silly as it would have seemed yesterday, I now realize this is my sign—my signal that this is it.

This is my starting point.

This is where I begin my soche seche tente.

In two days I will be back in the Takunami village.

In two days I will see Maha.

In two days . . . I will show Paho how wrong he was.

LUKA

12 Years, 362 Sunrises
The Amazon

Paho is dead. Impossible. The world is spinning and I grab the bench tighter. What am I going to do?

A thousand thoughts ricochet in my mind, making it impossible for me to focus. I know I will have to wait until Tukkita speaks to the spirit world. This is how the Takunami decide what to do with a boy whose father dies before he turns thirteen. In the past, the Good Gods have ordered boys to be abandoned and find their way home alone, or to be paired with their *paholo*, their father's father. One boy, Miniho, was taken five sunsets before his test, but given a bow, some arrows, and a knife to get home.

What will they do with me?

I look over at Tukkita, but his eyes are closed. I know not to disturb him when he is in a trance. Yet I must know what he has found out.

"Tukkita," I whisper.

The medicine man shows no sign he has heard me.

Wait. What did Tukkita say about Karara? He said she had been there when the Punhana appeared. So she had lived through the night. For the first time since learning about my father's death, I am thankful. My sister has not died because of my lie.

But what about the bird I heard that night? Did the Punhana follow Karara when she came back to see my father?

I stare at my mother, still passed out in her hammock. Maha was right; Karara is always causing trouble.

"She should have just stayed in the woods. She might be dead, but Paho would still be here."

"What are you saying, Luka?" Tukkita asks.

"Karara." I turn to face him. "This is her fault. She angered the forest spirits, and now they are punishing us. First she found out who Paho was, and then she led the Punhana to him when it was actually meant for her."

I expect him to be both surprised and angry, but he just shakes his head. "No, Luka. Your father did not die because of Karara. He actually lived longer because of her. There are some things you need to know."

The old man looks at me with eyes that are now clear. "Luka, your sister has a very special talent. Karara is a shaman . . . like myself."

Tukkita is the most respected man in our tribe, so I look down to hide my disbelief.

The shaman nods his head and sighs. "When I explained this to your mother, she had the same look." He pauses. "Your sister is very powerful, Luka. I have never seen healing powers like hers."

"She went where she didn't belong."

"*I* introduced her to your father. He had been sick for a long time, Luka. She was his only hope."

"Why would you do that, Tukkita?" I ask, my voice rising. "How could you betray my family? No Takunami girl has ever"—I stomp my foot—"*ever* known her father before her brother has. No one. Until now."

"The Good Gods did not kill your father, Luka. And neither did your sister."

"Then who? What killed him? Why did he die?"

The shaman is silent. Finally he speaks. "He was poisoned."

"Liar!" my mother screams. She is now sitting up and glaring at Tukkita.

"How dare you come into my hut and say these things? I want you out. *Now!*"

Tukkita does not move. "I have spoken no false words against you, Nunooma. I have only told Luka what he wanted to know—why his father died. And it is true, he was poisoned."

"Yes, by you and my daughter." My mother jabs a finger at him. "You poisoned him. By taking him to the river every day, you made him sicker and sicker. And I never would have known if I had not caught you that day of Luka's sight test."

"The Amazon was good for your husband. The female spirit of the river combined with the female energy of your daughter was the only thing that kept him alive."

I think back to the day I found the gate to the wash area unlocked. My mother must have surprised Paho and my sister as they were leaving the water. *They* were the ones who left the gate open.

"Then why did he die?" Maha asks. "If Karara is so powerful, why couldn't she save him?"

"Because you banished her from the village and by the time she came back, it was too late."

"What are you talking about?" I stand between Tukkita and my mother. "Why did Paho need female energy?"

My mother silently glowers at Tukkita.

"I will give you one chance to explain, Nunooma. Otherwise I will tell Luka what he has asked."

"You have no idea what you are saying." Maha storms toward the door. "I will not allow him to listen."

"One chance, Nunooma."

"*Mmpah,* Luka, let's go." She grabs my arm.

I pull it away and look at her. "Maha?"

"Your father was ill and Tukkita could not save him, so he is blaming me. That is what happened."

"That is one possibility, Luka," Tukkita says. "Now here is the other. When your mother gave birth to your older sister, she was very disappointed that Karara was a girl. She wanted only one child, the required son."

"Lies, all lies," my mother sputters.

Ignoring her, Tukkita continues. "When it came time to try again, Nunooma asked me for a potion to give your father. She was already drinking tea from the ku-ku-pa tree, but that had not worked with Karara, since she came out as a girl. So your mother wanted your father to take a potion also. When I refused, she took matters into her own hands. As you know, all plants and animals in the jungle are filled with a spirit. Even at a young age, your sister was showing signs of shamanism, so your mother made Karara gather plants from the jungle that contained the male spirit. Then your mother brewed all of these ingredients into a tea and gave it to your father every night for the next three months."

"And it worked, didn't it?" Maha laughs in the back of her throat. "The next child was Luka."

"Nine months later, you were born," Tukkita agrees, "and your father was very happy."

"Aha—" Maha begins.

"But," Tukkita interrupts, "not long after you began to crawl, he came to me because he did not feel well. He slept plenty, yet he was always tired. I gave him some bark to eat and he complained no more. Twelve moons after his first visit, he returned to me, limping. He laughed, saying he was getting old, but I could see something was wrong. Over the years, your father's body began to weaken—slowly and one part at a time—but soon he was unable to move without assistance. When I visited the spirit world for guidance, I had dreams of your sister picking plants. I asked her about this, and she told me what your mother had done."

I turn to Maha. "Is this true?"

"Yes. I did make a tea from the plants your sister brought back. But it was her fault your father got sick. She gave me the wrong leaves."

"All the male spirits that had been in the plants went to war when they entered your father's body," Tukkita continues. "There were too many, and they slowly killed each other off, taking your paho with them. There was nothing more I could do, so I asked Karara for help. It was she who came up with the idea of immersing your father in the female body of the Amazon to negate all the masculine energy."

My mind is spinning. *Karara didn't kill Paho.*

"If I hate children so much, Tukkita, why did I have Sulali?" my mother asks.

"You felt guilty. When you saw how sick Honati became, you knew it was your fault. He loved children, so you had another to keep him happy. The masculine spirits were so busy fighting each other, they didn't even stop long enough to give you another warrior. You had a baby girl."

I run to the door and gulp in fresh air. *My mother didn't kill Paho.*

"Enough, Tukkita . . ." My mother and the shaman continue to argue, but I no longer hear them.

I killed my father. In order for me to be born, my father had to die.

CHAPTER EIGHT

TIRIO

12 Years, 363 Days
The Amazon

A hundred yards in front of me a po-no sits rooted in a patch of mud. I aim for the beach and gun the boat's motor, praying it'll hold out a little longer. The engine kicks the boat forward with one last cough before dying, and we glide onto the bank.

When I jump out to anchor the rope, I realize I'm still wearing my socks and shoes. In order to pass the soche seche tente, a boy must return to the village the way he left it. I don't want my father to say I had help, so I remove my footwear and toss it into the boat. Now I'm ready.

Turning around, I take a deep breath and look at the tiny half circle of beach and the wall of trees surrounding it. I stride toward the woods, hoping to find a trail, but it's as if the trees have linked branches in a united front to keep me out. There's no choice but to wade along the bank and look for a way into the jungle.

The river is too muddy for me to see the bottom, so I grab a stick to measure the depth. Staying close to the shore, I pick my way along the bank. The water is deliciously cool against my legs, and I think back to when I was younger, playing in the wash area with the other kids. After finishing the laundry, my mother would stand at the beach, hands on hips, and frown at the mass of swimming children. Grinning at her frustration, I would tread water and wait. Finally, unable to pick me out, she'd throw her hands up and yell, "Tirio, *mmpah*—let's go!" It wasn't until I was back on the shore that she could tell by the footstep-drag-footstep that, yes, I was her son.

I stop and turn to look at the beach behind me. A pair of well-shaped footprints are stamped into the mud. Thunder rumbles close by and I look up to see menacing clouds overhead. A few raindrops freckle the water as I hurry forward, desperate to find a way into the protection of the jungle before the sky opens completely.

Inching along, I think how stupid I was to look for a trail from the beach. Of course no animals would go to such an open spot to drink. It would be too dangerous. With their heads down, they'd be vulnerable to predators. They would want to stay camouflaged in the jungle. *You've got to start thinking like a Takunami!* I silently scold myself as the rain starts to fall harder.

I'm about fifty yards from the beach when suddenly I can't find the river bottom with my stick. I turn toward the shore and see a narrow trail in the brush. Realizing where I am, I yelp and quickly pull myself up onto the bank. Scrambling away from the water, I run into the jungle, trying to get away from the shore. When I feel I'm far enough, I stop and, with my eyes, follow the trail back to the river. I'm not worried about the storm anymore. If I'm right—and I'm pretty sure I am—I just stumbled into a caiman's underwater den.

The lazy reptile had parked himself right by the trail, so when some thirsty animal came for a drink, he could just snap it up. Little work, big reward. Shivering, I hurry away in the opposite direction.

The path is narrow, and in some spots the crawling vines and plants devour it so completely, I think it has ended. But after pushing some branches aside, and trampling some brush, I see it beckoning a couple of yards ahead. The jungle will take back an unused trail within days, but luckily, at least one large animal is consistently using this one.

I keep my eyes and ears open for signs I need to change directions. After the caimans, I feel confident that the Good Gods will show me the way.

Suddenly, I freeze. What was that? I crouch. A chill

runs down my spine. There it is again . . . a piercing screech. Where did it come from? Scanning the nearby trees, I spot a *kaka-ta* parakeet huddled on a low-hanging branch. Its feathers are soggy and limp, and it hangs its head and wails again.

Birds are the built-in alarm system of the jungle, and the Takunami use them as signals of danger. I grab a nearby stick and try to figure out what is happening. I peer through the blanket of rain until finally I see a flash of movement. A fat *prupita* glares at me from its position a foot off the trail. The lizard flicks its tongue but doesn't retreat. The parakeet moans again. The bright green feathers lying around and the remnants of a fallen nest tell me the story: the prupita has attacked the nest and eaten the parakeet's babies.

I wipe my rain-plastered hair out of my eyes. The prupita isn't blocking the path, so I decide it's not a sign to stop. I step cautiously around the tree and hurry forward.

I think about the poor parakeet mother, and then I think about my own. I wonder what *she* did when she got back to the village the day I left? Did she continue with the rest of her chores: weaving baskets, planting new vegetables, cleaning the hut? Did she brood, moaning and hanging her head like the parakeet? I frown. What do I *wish* she had done?

I hope that after mourning for a respectable amount of time, she went back to living life—and was happy.

But what's a respectable amount of time? A month? Six months? A year?

How long did she wait to have another son? Did she tell him about me?

There is an offshoot of a trail ahead and, although no sign from the Good Gods points the way, I decide to veer toward it.

NO! DON'T! TURN AROUND! DANGER! STOP!

The force of the thoughts is so strong, I grab my temples and stagger backward. I know the voice is right. An unshakable hunch has taken over my whole body—a familiar hunch, I realize, growing cold—a hunch just like the one I had on the soccer field.

YOU MUST TURN AROUND! THIS IS NOT THE WAY.

I spin in a circle, looking for him. This is it. My father has started communicating with me. He's just taken over, like a puppeteer.

Knowing that what I'm about to do may be stupid, I grit my teeth and continue along the offshoot. *Sorry,*

Paho, but if my body wasn't good enough for you seven years ago, then it's not good enough now. I need to do this on my own.

LISTEN TO ME. YOU DO NOT KNOW WHAT YOU ARE DOING.

I run, but with each step, his thoughts pound harder against my skull.

YOU NEED MY HELP. YOU CAN'T DO THIS ON YOUR OWN. STOP!

I try to think about other things to block him out. I start to sing the alphabet song in my head.

A, B, C, D, E, F, G . . .

NO. NO! NO! he roars.

. . . H, I, J, K, L, M, N, O, P . . .

TURN AROUND.

. . . Q, R, S . . .

BAD.

. . . T, U, V . . .

I can see the original path.

. . . W, X, Y, and Z.

STOP.

Now I know my ABC's . . .

I'm at the intersection of the trails.

Silence.

Next time won't you sing . . .

I hold my breath.

. . . with . . .

My eyes dart around.

. . . me.

Silence.

He's gone.

My head is pounding like I just got smacked with twenty soccer balls, but I force myself to continue sprinting ahead, *not* the way *he* wants me to go. The rain hammers me, and I stop and raise my mouth to the sky. The water trickles down my parched throat, but it's not enough. Then I see a grove of plantains. Their leaves, as big as elephant ears, catch the rain and empty it onto the ground like the gutter on a roof. Positioning myself under one of the leaves, I let the rain pour into my mouth. I stop to catch my breath and then drink more. Luck stays with me. The tree has ripe fruit and, jumping up, I grab a few plantains. I ignore the lingering headache and continue.

After a while, another small path appears to my right and a tiny arrow of green on the ground points me toward it—a sign from the Good Gods as bright as if painted with neon. I kneel and shake my head at this amazing assembly line of insects. Holding leaves ten times their size like umbrellas, millions of *bu-ki* ants scurry toward their colony. I jump when I notice I'm standing in the middle of their route. Leaning over to check out the damage I've caused, I wince at the several wounded ants in my footprint. A couple struggle to recover, and one, having never let go of his load, limps along, leaving a leg behind. I watch as his comrades step over and on top of him without slowing. I pick up the leaf with him still clinging to it, and place it next to the ant hole. I watch him safely disappear inside. First the parakeet and now this—I'd forgotten how cruel nature is.

The rain finally stops, and I'm thankful for the break. Fingering machete marks on the vines, I look around cautiously. No one has been here for a couple of days, judging by the absence of footprints, but I have to stay alert. Not all tribes are friendly to visitors, especially when the visitors are males.

Cupping my hand around the back of my ear, I listen. A couple of miles east, a peccary chews tree bark. To the north, an anteater vacuums a dinner of termites. To the west, a capybara drinks from a puddle, and to the south I hear a parrot caw to its mate.

I continue to jog until a new trail appears, and I listen again.

East: A family of otters munches on fish.

North: Two male lemon monkeys fight for a female's attention.

West: I frown. Closing my eyes, I erase my mind of any thoughts and hone my whole body into hearing. It can't be. There is a *pu-la* deer searching for a place to nap, but beyond that. . . . I place my other hand in front of my ear and form an uninterrupted tunnel toward the sound. I lean sideways, holding my breath. It is very distant—many miles away—but what I hear is a woman singing.

I can't make out the words, but the rhythm seems familiar. Is it Maha? Is she trying to lead me home? I strain to hear clearer, hoping to recognize something familiar in the voice. I can't and I realize, even though it might be dangerous, I have to check it out. Feeling strangely like a rat being led by the Pied Piper, I follow the sound of the song.

LUKA

12 Years, 363 Sunrises
The Amazon

When I wake, I'm not sure of the time, the day, or even where I am, but as I look around, it comes back to me. Today should be the first day of my soche seche tente. Instead I am lying in my hut, staring at a spider scurrying across the ceiling.

My father will not be communicating with me through the sixth sense. I will never hear him or speak with him. Today, I will meet him for the first time. Today, I will meet him for the last time. It is a day when I should jump up and get going. Instead, I feel as though someone has roped me to the hammock.

I hear the shuffling of feet and turn to see Sulali staring at me. I don't have answers to the questions in her eyes. I told her we would all be a happy family, that soon she would meet her paho. Only a five-year-old would look to a liar for answers a second time—only a five-year-

136

old and someone who doesn't have anyone else to believe.

I manage a smile. "Come here, Sulali. Don't worry. Paho would have wanted us to be strong in front of the rest of the tribe, so we have to stick together."

"How can we without Karara?" She climbs in next to me.

"Didn't you hear?" As I shift over to make room for her, a story starts forming in my head. I can't stand to see my little sister suffer anymore.

"Hear what?"

"What happened to Karara?"

"No." Sulali's voice shakes, and I know I'm making the right decision.

I put my arm around her. "She's not here because she is on a very important mission."

"A mission?"

"Yesterday when Karara was with Paho, she saw the Punhana too."

Sulali sucks in her breath when I mention the bird of death.

"Since Karara is a shaman, she could speak with the bird, so she tried to talk him out of taking Paho." I am amazed how easily the lie is coming out.

I soften my voice to sound like a girl. "'Take me instead, Punhana,' Karara said to the bird. 'I am worth much more because I have magic powers and can help you.'"

I lower my voice to mimic what I think the wise old bird would sound like. "'Magic powers mean nothing to me,' the Punhana replied. 'I want the man. It is he who I was sent for and it is he whose spirit I must return with.'"

I pause, and Sulali nudges closer to me. I turn my body to face her and stare at the shadows cast by the rising sun on the ground in front of our hut. The branches and vines from the forest form mysterious shapes as they intersect, and I use them to tell my story. "Look, Sulali, the Good Gods are showing you how it happened." I point to the dirt.

She swings her gaze. The silhouette of a woman walks by, and she gasps. I quickly make my voice high and continue.

"'Why must you take my paho? Why is he so important?' Karara asked."

"'This man belongs in the heavens with the other high spirits. He has fulfilled his purpose.'"

A twig cracks behind our hut, and I freeze. No other sound follows. I wonder who's listening out there. Is it just Maha? Or could it be Karara?

"What was Paho's purpose?" asks Sulali.

"You really want to know?" I ask.

"Yes."

"Well, so did Karara, so she asked the Punhana. 'What purpose has my father fulfilled, and why isn't he able to stay with his family?'

"'Your father was a great warrior and fought many tribes before you were born. However, on one war expedition, his arrow flew through the enemy and into a woman.'"

Sulali snorts. "Why was the woman standing behind a warrior during a battle?"

"It was the man's wife," I answer. "She was pregnant and he was protecting her."

Sulali nods, satisfied, and I continue. "Our father felt so bad about killing the woman and child that he asked the Good Gods to spare the child's life in return for his own.

"So Karara said to the bird, 'I don't understand, Punhana. Why didn't the Good Gods agree? A great warrior's life in exchange for a child seems like a good trade.'

"'They did agree,' the bird said. 'But first your father had to create another family for this child because his family was dead. So your paho was told to return to the Takunami and have three children, two daughters and a son—'"

Sulali elbowed me. "Is that you, me, and Karara?"

139

With my ear still tuned to the noises outside, I answer yes. "Once the family was formed, the orphan would come and live with us, and our father would have to fulfill his end of the promise and die," I tell Sulali.

Her lips tilt down into a frown at this turn of events, but I continue with the story.

"'But where is the boy?' Karara asked the bird."

I lower my voice to sound like the Punhana again. "'You must find him,' the bird said. 'As the oldest, it is your job to bring the boy home. When I leave, you should go and look for him. I will take care of your father's spirit. I will set it free.' And with that the Punhana flew away, and Karara followed him into the jungle to search for the orphan."

The silhouette of a low-flying bird flashes by, and Sulali squeals. I am amazed at the kindness of the Good Gods.

"Maybe Tambo knows where the boy is," she whispers. "I'll ask him."

"Good idea." I ease out of the hammock. Someone is outside. I just know it.

I step into the sunlight. Leaning over, I search for clues in the dirt.

"What are you doing?" Sulali asks from inside the hut.

Not wanting to disappoint her in case the someone

isn't Karara, I quickly think of a lie.

"I'm trying to track Tambo's prints so you can go look for him."

"Oh." Her voice is filled with excitement. I hear her feet hit the ground as she hops out of the hammock.

"Stay inside, Sulali," I order. "I don't want you to mess up the trail."

Seeing what I think are my older sister's footprints, I follow the trail around the hut. It disappears into the men's rohacas.

"Karara?" I whisper.

Maha strides by with a bucket of water. She stops when she sees me. "What are you doing?"

I straighten. "Nothing."

She motions me back to our hut.

Drumbeats in the distance signal that a ceremony will soon take place. *Bam, bam.* Pause. *Bam, bam, bam.* Pause, pause. *Bam.*

The funeral. By now, everyone knows Paho is dead.

There are certain times in the Takunami life when we mark our bodies with dye to symbolize an important change: weddings, soche seche tente ceremonies, and funerals. Sometimes women will also add flowers to their hair, or men will wear beaded leather ropes around their waists, but the small red marks of the *gi-gi* berry are traditional. For a wedding, a circle is drawn on the skin above the man's and woman's hearts; when a boy becomes a warrior, his whole face is painted red; during a funeral, the eyelids of the family and the dead are painted. The color of the gi-gi dye is the same as blood: blood being shared between man and woman, blood being shifted from father to son, and blood being lost from a family.

Maha must have picked the berries on her morning trip; I see them as soon as I walk inside. I grab some and call Sulali over. As I squeeze the juice onto my finger and then onto my sister's eyelids, I cannot help but think how differently I was supposed to wear this red color in a couple of days.

My sister and I wait outside until Maha is ready, and then the three of us walk together toward the center of the village. Sulali holds my hand and, for once, I walk slowly enough for her to keep up.

In typical Takunami fashion, my father's body will be burned, and it is our job to place him on top of the fire. My eyes search the jungle, hoping that Karara will rush out and fall into step with us.

Tukkita is standing close to the flames, but I know he does not feel the heat. In preparation for the ceremony, he has inhaled a mixture of sacred leaves and bark that allows him to communicate with the spirits. He has tied a large rock to his wrist with a vine, to keep his body grounded to this world while his soul travels. His eyes are closed and sweat trickles over his bony rib cage. The other tribe members chat in hushed tones but fall silent as we approach.

My father has been wrapped in a colorful blanket that signals a warrior of high standing. I think about my story to Sulali; maybe it wasn't that far off.

When I reach the opening of the circle, I release Sulali's hand and walk forward alone. As the son, I must uncover my father's face. Doing so will allow his eyes to see the release of his spirit. It is said that a dead person's eyes will flash open the moment before his soul reunites with the spirit world.

My hands are shaking as I pull back the cloth and, for the first time, lay eyes on my father. My heart sinks. He is not the strong and handsome man I hoped he would be. He is as thin as Tukkita, with a mouth puckered into a sunken circle and hair the color of an old bone. He is a man I have seen only a few times in the village, someone I took to be a paholo. I would have never walked by him and tried to find a family resemblance, yet as I tuck the cloth under his waist, I see where I got my large hands. *He looks kind,* I remind myself, and if what Tukkita said was true, he was a very good person.

Knowing that many are watching, including Sulali, I keep my expression blank, walk around to my father's head, and reach under the board that holds him. Maha steps forward and moves to his feet. Sulali stands in the center. Tukkita sings in a shaky moan, and we carry my father's body to the fire. The shaman breaks into a series of low and high pitches. When he begins to moan again, my mother and I lift the board over our heads and then down onto the blazing logs. The flames greedily eat at the wood, fiber, and flesh. Tukkita throws his head back like an angry cat and begins to howl. Sparks snap around us, and I am thankful for the smell of the eucalyptus we burn with the body.

"Come this way," Tukkita sings.

The rest of the tribe tightens the circle, which prevents evil spirits from interrupting the reunion of soul and spirit.

"Come this way."

The fire reaches higher, making it easier for my father's sick body to complete his journey. Without warning, the wind shifts and the flames suddenly lunge at us with red and yellow crooked fingers. Sulali whimpers and hides her face behind my arm. Closing my eyes halfway, I force myself to stand tall, not even flinching as floating pieces of ash land on my skin. Next to me, Maha stands as rooted as an old po-no. For once, I'm grateful for her stubbornness.

"Let go of your body, trust in your soul, open your eyes, and come this way."

I jerk my head around. Another voice has joined the howling of Tukkita. It is Karara. Her short hair is slicked back with tonka oil, and tears flow down her upturned face. Maha glares at her. Sulali tries to wiggle her hand free from mine, but I tighten my grip and look back at my father's body.

"Come this way." Karara sings the song of the spirits in a strong voice. "Do not be afraid. Open your eyes and come this way."

Almost on cue, my father's eyes open. Glancing up, I look for his soul, but see nothing. By the time I look back down, his eyes have closed. It didn't take long for his soul to find the spirits. It didn't take long at all.

CHAPTER NINE

TIRIO

12 Years, 363 Days
The Amazon

The song leads me down the path then suddenly seems to stop. A rumble in the distance signals another storm and I hurry forward, desperate not to lose the voice. As the wind whips my hair, I cup my hand around my ear. I shiver as the strong breeze brings the singing back to me. It is the Takunami funeral song.

Thunder booms above me and I start to jog toward the woman's voice.

Suddenly, my skin erupts into goose bumps and I freeze. There is another sound. I hold my breath.

Padding paws. An animal. *A jaguar.*

The jaguar is the only animal my tribe never hunts or kills; we believe the spirits of our dead shamans live on in this sacred cat. The only problem is, this jaguar might not have the soul of a Takunami. It could be that of an enemy.

The shadows of the forest have disappeared. Nightfall will soon make it impossible for me to see. Looking for a way to escape the cat's path, I notice a heart palm on the trail in front of me. If I climb it, the jaguar might turn toward easier prey on the ground.

Crack! A blinding whiteness explodes around me and a great force flattens me to the jungle floor. The earth vibrates underneath me and I scramble behind a bush and pull my knees into my chest. I smell smoke. What was that? Are the Good Gods trying to punish me? Was the singing a trap?

The hairs on my arms stand at attention; the air is filled with an electricity so heavy I could cup it in my hands. Hearing the flapping of wings, I peek around the bush and see a bright green *tooka* fly through the air toward me and then continue down the trail. *"Wee-wee-o,"* it calls, beckoning me. *"Wee-wee-o."* I take a small step and peek out onto the path, gasping when I see what caused the explosion: a tree got hit by lightning. And not just any tree, but the heart palm I had thought about climbing. When I realize what would have happened if I had been here a little earlier, or the lightning had struck a little later . . . my body turns cold.

I tiptoe forward, stepping over the burning pieces of forest until I'm standing at the base of a smoldering tree.

The beetle grubs that were living inside ooze out like they're the tree's intestines. My stomach rumbles and I hesitate only a second longer before stuffing a handful into my mouth. Warm and soft, they taste like cheese, and I remember how excited I used to be when we harvested them. Quickly, I swallow and grab more.

Seeing a palm frond burning in front of me, I realize this tree *is* going to save me from the jaguar after all. A fire would be the perfect way to keep the cat away, and I've got a huge lit match right in front of me. As the rain starts to pour, I break branches off nearby trees and rip down clinging vines, placing them on top of the already flaming leaves. Shoving more grubs into my mouth, I shield the newly smoldering wood with other fronds until they too are ablaze. Then I set out for more. The fire devours everything, growing higher and lighting up the surrounding forest. I make ten more trips for wood, widening my search and snatching everything within reach. Suddenly, the jaguar howls again, closer this time. Clutching the sticks to my chest, I hurry back to the safety of the tree.

Eyeing the pile of wood I've collected, I calculate that if I only use two or three pieces every couple of hours, I'll have enough to make it through the night. It won't be a roaring bonfire, but it should be enough to keep the cat away. I circle the fire with stones, to keep it from spreading, and then bow my head. *Thank you, Good Gods.*

Squish, squish, squish, squish. The jaguar's padded paws steadily approach.

I drop one end of a stick into the red ash; a flaming poker will be extra protection.

Swoosha, swoosha, swoosha. Her slow, rhythmic heartbeat tells me she's in no hurry.

Suddenly, she stops and scratches the forest floor. Judging from the volume of her movements, it sounds like she's still quite a way away. Sighing, she lies down and begins to purr.

I pace around the fire, confused by her actions. What jaguar acts like this? Why did she stop stalking me? I pull the stick-poker out of the fire and nod at its glowing tip before propping it between my feet. Feeling confident by her distance and slow breathing that she won't charge, I sit with my back against a tree. As the adrenaline drains from my body and the fire warms my wet clothes, the exhaustion that I've been outrunning all day finally catches up to me. Leaning my head back against the wet bark of the tree, I think about home.

Joey. By now the bomb has been dropped on him; he knows about his parents' divorce. I wonder how he's doing. Did he go to the soccer field and smash balls into the goal like he always does when he's mad? I wonder what I should say to him when I get home. Dropping my head in my hands, I try to imagine how I would want to be treated. My mind is a big blank hole and after opening my eyes again, I decide to ask Sara.

Sara. What did she do after she read my letter? Cry? No, that's not her style. I bet she immediately ran out and started looking for me—her and Juan Diego, yelling my name, riding up and down the river. I stare at the smoke still coming out of the heart palm. I hope Juan Diego convinced her to wait until the storm passed and it was safe.

Nothing had better happen to her.

The rain has slowed to a mist and I hug my knees for warmth, staring without blinking into the flames. Forms dance in the flickering embers—a parakeet, a lizard, giant ants marching. I watch the dance until my eyes get so dry, I have to close them. It feels so good that I decide to keep them shut awhile longer, only for a short time. Just a few minutes.

I wake up cold and shivering. A light drizzle continues to fall and all around me the forest is dark. My fire is dead. Jumping up, I grab the smallest twigs and bark from my woodpile. When I blow on the gray ashes, I'm relieved to see a flicker of red blink back. I coax it with tiny pieces of dead fern, stoking the flames to life. Dumb, dumb, dumb! How could I have fallen asleep? The chill from the ground has seeped into my bones. I clench my jaw to keep my teeth from chattering and crouch by the slowly recovering fire.

The hairs on the back of my neck prickle as I listen for the jaguar. Her steady breathing assures me she hasn't moved.

The moon shines through the gap where the burning palm once stood. My senses sound a warning: I'm being watched. Turning, I peer into the darkness.

SOMETHING IS THERE. My father's voice pushes into my thoughts. He is back.

I promised myself not to take his help. *Go away,* I think. *I don't need you here.*

LOOK . . . LISTEN . . . SMELL. His voice is filled with urgency.

I know what to do. I don't need him to tell me.

THIS IS NO TRICK. HE WILL KILL YOU.

I reach for the burning poker I propped between my feet earlier. It has burned down to the size of a cigar, so I throw it back and grab the top piece of wood from my stash. Rotten, it breaks in two. I seize another stick and spin around, searching the jungle.

I sniff. There is no wind, but the rain makes every scent easy to pick up. Whatever is approaching is not human. It's an animal. A big animal. Another jaguar—a male. I circle the fire, hoping to keep it between myself and the cat.

"Yeow!" The female is awake and running toward me, but the male is closer. I pick up the vibrations from his vocal cords before they even become a sound. They form a growl so low and deep, it enters my body through my feet.

"Yeow!" The female howls again. She is running at full tilt.

I DON'T KNOW WHO HE IS. THE CAT IS NOT A TAKUNAMI SHAMAN.

My mind is reeling.

HE WANTS YOU. STAY CLOSE TO THE FIRE. STIR IT. YOU WILL SEE HIS EYES.

I didn't ask you, I shoot back angrily, rotating around the fire and stirring up the flames. I would have done this anyway.

I can feel the animal . . . behind me. Looking over my shoulder, I see two glaring eyes. The cat is watching my every move.

A flash of lightning illuminates the forest. I stop

breathing. Crouched ten feet away from me is a black jaguar as big as two grown men.

Frozen, I watch the male jaguar stride forward.

"Go away!" I wave my stick. "Get out of here!"

The animal stalks toward me, oblivious to the flames. Fat raindrops land on my head and arms as I back around the fire. The storm is not over.

Lightning. Thunder. I see a brown and black mottled shape fly though the air. The female jaguar. And then I run. Looking back, I see them rolling around the fire, jaws snapping to reach that soft spot on the neck that will end it.

The sky opens into a downpour.

THE TRAIL SPLITS AHEAD. TAKE THE PATH THAT VEERS RIGHT.

I see the fork he's talking about.

IT'S THE LONGER PATH TO THE VILLAGE, BUT IT'LL BE EASIER FOR YOUR FOOT, my father continues. *CAN YOU MAKE IT, SON?*

Son? My face burns at what he just said. How dare he call me *Son.* And why is he faking concern for me? After deciding I wasn't strong enough to waste effort on seven years ago, he's trying to make things *easier* for me now?

TIRIO? My father's voice sounds worried.

Forget it, I think, narrowing my eyes and picking up my pace. *Too little too late, Paho.* And then without even slowing down—without even hesitating—I ignore him and go straight.

LUKA

12 Years, 364 Sunrises
The Amazon

The rain pounds the roof of our hut like an angry woman beating an old frond rug. I lie in my hammock and feel the thunder shake the ground. Usually I sleep my best during storms, but last night I couldn't even close my eyes. Yesterday at the funeral, when Karara stopped singing, the Good Gods clapped their approval in the form of thunder and opened up the sky. The storms lasted all night, teasing us with short breaks before returning for a second, a third, a fourth time. Lightning illuminates the room and I see the shapes of Maha and Sulali in their hammocks.

Thunder again, but this time it's in the distance; the storm is retreating. I rise and open the door. Pausing, I leave it cracked and tiptoe to Sulali's hammock. A braid has fallen across her cheek and I brush it away. She has not let anyone touch her hair since Karara left, and it now lies knotted and dirty across her pillow. Her father is dead and her sister is gone. If something happens to me, her only family left will be Maha, a woman who has never once played with her daughter. I can't do that to Sulali. I hope the spirits don't ask me to.

Tukkita's hut is located down a winding path, isolated from the village. It is where the shaman before Tukkita lived and where the next one will too. The next one—that will be Karara. If she ever comes home. I feel my sister's presence as I walk up to the hut. I pray that she's here. I need to talk to her—to apologize, to find out what our father was like, to convince her to resolve things with Maha. After the funeral, she disappeared into the crowd and I never had a chance.

Sensing I'm outside his door, Tukkita pokes his head out and beckons me in. I step through the doorway.

"Karara is not here," the shaman says.

I look at the ground.

"You are early for our meeting," he says, walking toward a table and turning his back to me.

"I want to begin," I explain, following him.

He doesn't respond, and I tiptoe around the fire to peek over his shoulder. On top of the table, I see a wooden bowl containing black powder and four short, hollow pieces of bamboo.

Tukkita shoves some powder into one of the bamboo pieces.

"What are you doing?" I ask.

Reaching down, he picks something up and slips it over my wrist. It's a vine attached to the leg of the table. "You are about to see your future, Luka," he says. I suck in my breath. *Me?* Someone my age is usually not allowed to perform this ritual.

Sensing my hesitation, Tukkita stops packing the powder to explain. "When a boy's father dies before he has completed his test, I turn to the spirit world for advice. I was unable to see anything except a vision of you. They want to speak to you."

After the bowl is empty, Tukkita separates the bamboo pieces into two sets. For the first time, I notice they are different sizes. "These are mine," he says, pointing to the bigger ones. "These are yours." He hands me a smaller one.

"Put this inside your nose and take a deep breath," he instructs. "When I'm sure you've done it correctly, then I will go. We will each go twice."

I shudder, remembering how Tukkita looks after doing this type of ritual—groaning and drooling and trembling as though he's in terrible pain—but I nod and take the bamboo. I have no choice. Squeezing my eyes shut, I pinch one nostril shut and inhale quickly through the other before I can change my mind. Like powdered fire, the mixture explodes in my nose and then claws its way down the back of my throat.

I hear Tukkita's familiar wail and turn to focus on him. He's doubled over, a large empty bamboo in his hand. "Go again," he commands hoarsely.

I lurch for the table. The room is spinning as I grab a piece of bamboo and quickly snort the contents. The second time, my nose burns as badly as the first. I gag as last night's dinner rises into my throat and spit on the floor, but the acidic taste of the black powder remains. My body numbs and I close my eyes. I feel as though I'm floating.

A quietness surrounds me and I open my eyes to see my spirit drifting above my body. Tukkita is below me, shaking his head and holding the last bamboo piece. It's one of the small ones and I realize what I did wrong.

Within a few minutes, the shaman is soaring next to me. He grabs my hand roughly. "No more mistakes, Luka. Close your eyes."

My stomach rolls and my head pounds and I stare at

the back of my eyelids. Nothing is happening and I pinch my eyes tighter. Finally, from the right corner of the blackness, I see myself emerge holding hands with a young girl. Her walk is graceful but tentative and she bows her head away from me. She grips a bouquet of orchids so tightly the juice from the stems drips down her wrist. We walk toward Tukkita and, although I cannot hear what he is saying, I recognize the mark of the gi-gi berry he is placing above our hearts. We are getting married.

The scene fades to darkness and then opens to a picture of my wife washing clothes in the river. Her back is to me, but when she turns, I see she is clutching her stomach. I gasp. Her belly is round with child. The scenes flash by quickly, but I can tell by the change of day to night to day again, the birth was difficult. I see myself holding the baby, kissing him on the forehead and handing him back to his mother. Only then do I realize I still have not seen her face.

My wife leans over our little boy as he learns to walk. He grips her thumbs with chubby fingers and tries to balance between her legs. They are both smiling as they inch across a dirt floor.

Next, my son totters in the grass, moving away from my wife, who crouches nearby protectively. But something is wrong. My wife scoops him up and hugs him as someone approaches. It is Tukkita. He speaks to her as my son laughs and pulls her earrings. After Tukkita leaves, tears begin to flow down my wife's cheeks. She buries her face in her hand and her shoulders shake. Our little boy also covers his face, and giggles.

There is a crowd of children running. One falls behind. He is limping. He stops. It is my son. My wife appears from nowhere and scurries away with him.

My wife hides behind a tree. She is listening to the shaman and me speak. She raises clenched fists to the sky.

I wait for another picture. Tukkita releases my hand. "That is all. We are finished. Open your eyes."

But we are not finished.

"Luka, open your eyes!" Tukkita yells from below. *"Luka. Now. Open your eyes."* I hear him but do not listen. I am still floating, and another scene appears. I watch.

The Amazon carries a canoe in its current. My child lies inside. A woman with white skin pulls the limp child from the boat. It is my son. He is dead. No . . . he reaches up and clutches her neck. He is alive.

Blackness.

"Luka!"

I am standing on the dirt floor of the shaman's hut.

"What happened?" Tukkita is so close, his nose touches mine.

My mouth feels like I've swallowed a sloth and I can barely pull my lips apart to ask for water. Tukkita hands me a cup.

"Nothing," I lie.

"What did you see after I left?"

Leaning against a wall, I try to keep my body from shaking. My head is pounding and I don't know whether it is from the potion or from seeing my life play out in front of me.

"Swirling colors. I was hoping there would be more, so I waited."

I quickly cover my face with the cup.

"Was there anything more?"

"No." My voice is muffled by the wood.

I can feel him glaring at me. "I am sure you have questions."

I finish the water and ask for more. Drinking slowly, I give myself time to think. "What do the visions mean?" I finally ask him.

Tukkita pokes the fire and narrows his eyes as sparks fly around him. "It has been decided that rather than take your soche seche tente, you will marry and have a son."

I wait for him to continue, but instead, he walks to the door and motions me out.

Not moving, I beg him to tell me more. "Tukkita?" I plead.

Still silent, he points a finger back toward the village. Does he know I didn't tell him the truth about what I saw?

Sighing, I do as he asks, but stop in front of him. Keeping my voice steady, I ask, "When will I marry?"

"Tomorrow, on your thirteenth birthday. Instead of meeting your father, you will join lives."

"And the girl?" I ask. "Who's the girl?"

He cocks his head as if listening to something in the wind. Finally, he nods and gives me a small smile. "Maroma. Your future wife is Maroma."

CHAPTER TEN

TIRIO

12 Years, 364 Days
The Amazon

Going against my sixth-sense instinct is the hardest thing I've ever done. It's like I'm drowning, but instead of swimming up toward air, I make myself swim deeper toward the darkness. It feels wrong, and yet I keep doing it. I shut off my brain, shut off my senses, and go.

When the sun comes up, I realize I'm halfway done. By this time tomorrow, I have to be in the village. Excitement pumps through me, mixed with a little worry. So far I've been able to do everything without my father's help, but that might have forced me to take a harder way. I think I can make it, but can I make it in time?

I stop to drink from a water vine, then continue running. The monkeys and parakeets quiet as I approach and then screech after me like angry school crossing guards. I continue using my five senses to search for signs of my tribe—footprints, the smells of food or fire, the sounds of humans. The Good Gods have not sent me any more signals, so I just keep running and assume they will help if I need it.

My father keeps trying to communicate. Each time I pause, he pleads with me to listen. The more he pushes, the more I pull back. But he refuses to give up.

The rest of the morning we battle. A hunch from him pulls me to a trail on the left. I head right. He calls after me, telling me there will be fruit to eat up ahead, but I ignore him and stay on the path I'm on. There's more than one way to my village. Finally, I'm the one with the power.

By midafternoon, the rain has stopped and the sun pushes through the dense leaves to celebrate with me. I stop and drink again. Without the rain, the mosquitoes swarm me. I swat at them, but they won't leave. Each one buzzes with a question: *Why is it so important to him that I return? What if he's dying? What if he's the chief of the tribe and I'm his only son? Who was the funeral for? Is Maha okay? What if she never had any other males?*

I reach up and grab a *chu-chu* nut from a tree behind me. I don't want to talk to him, but I want to know how she is doing. I crack the nut and chew in frustration, then scream at the sky. A family of spider monkeys stares at me like I'm the newest attraction at the circus. Confusion Boy. And maybe I am. Step right up, ladies and gentlemen, and watch him beat his head against the trees.

Finally, I decide to end my silence with my father— not to ask for help, just to find out about Maha. *How is she?* I ask him. *Is she okay?* I wait for a response. *Please, just tell me if she's okay.*

My father doesn't answer. Why should he? I have been ignoring him for the past day and a half. What if he put these doubts in my mind? I can't even trust my thoughts anymore. I don't know what's real and what isn't.

The sun is setting and I shudder as my sweat dries to a chill. It will be dark soon, and suddenly not having a plan doesn't seem like the wonderful idea it was a couple of hours ago—especially now that my foot is aching too. The first twinges of pain started this morning, but I was able to ignore them. Now, after hours of no rest and no orthotic, my foot is letting me know it's not happy.

YOU ARE IN PAIN. IS IT YOUR FOOT?

No, my foot is fine . . . better than fine . . . fantastic.

YOU MUST TRUST ME. PLEASE LISTEN TO WHAT I AM TELLING YOU.

Why? I ask him. *Why should I listen to you?*

I UNDERSTAND THAT YOU ARE ANGRY, BUT WE HAVE TO WORK TOGETHER. WE ARE CLOSE,

165

BUT THERE IS NOT MUCH TIME.

What do you mean there isn't much time? Is something wrong with Maha?

Suddenly, the hairs on my neck stand up at familiar attention. It can't be, but it is. A low growl. The jaguar is back. Not the female, but the black one. I hear him behind me. I smell his breath. I feel his eyes focusing on the pulsing vein on the side of my neck. The pieces of *chu-chu* nut stick in my throat. I don't know what else to do . . . so I run. The cat follows, close enough that I know he's there, but far enough to make me think I have a chance.

COME HOME. LISTEN TO ME, ENOUGH IS ENOUGH.

Forget it. But even as I think it, I find myself obeying him. The forest has gotten dark, the cat is still behind me, and the jungle crowds me on either side. I'm running for my life. *I don't want to die*, I think as I race farther into the depths of the jungle.

YOU WON'T. He steers me like a car—left, left, and then right. My five senses are on alert. I feel like I do with my soccer team when we're on a roll, how we know each other so well that we can get a ball down the field effortlessly with only a few nods and eye gestures. Nobody ever brags about those moments after they happen, but we all know how special they are. As I run now, with my father guiding me, I feel that same magic. We're on the same team and we're both trying to get the same ball to the same goal. Me. Home. I can't say no to that.

The cat screams, and my father encourages me. *FASTER; HE IS VERY CLOSE. YOU MUST MOVE FASTER.*

I speed up, but my right foot suddenly spasms. I cry out. This can't be happening, not now; not after I've come so far. I clench my jaw and favor my left foot.

Ignore the pain, I think.

TIRIO, YOU MUST PUSH YOURSELF.

I do. I push myself harder than in any soccer game or any physical therapy session, but after another half hour, the throbbing has spread from my foot to my hip.

TIRIO!

I'm trying!

TRY HARDER.

I struggle to tune out the warning signs from my body. *Don't give up. Mind over matter, T. Go, go, go.*

YOU CAN DO THIS. I KNOW YOU CAN. His words are whispered, yet forceful.

It hurts. It hurts so badly.

Step, limp. Step, limp. I'm slowing down and, like any stalked prey, I feel the tide turn. So does my father.

*LISTEN TO ME. YOU ARE ALMOST HERE.
FOCUS ON MY VOICE. FOCUS ON THE END. YOU
HAVE TO DO THIS. YOU MUST MAKE IT. FOR
BOTH OF US.*

"I . . . don't . . . owe . . . you . . . anything." My words
come out in jagged sobs, and I feel myself growing angry
again. *"Nothing . . . do you hear me?"* I scream the sentence
rather than think it. "It's you . . . who . . . owes . . . me!"

Silence.

The cat is gaining ground. His feet pound the forest
floor, filling the spaces between my heartbeats.

"You . . . who . . . owes . . . me." Unable to run any
farther, I limp, and tears blur the path.

*The cat. The cat. The cat. The cat. The frog. The frog.
The frog. The frog.* I stop and bend over in pain. For the
second time in a week, I think about my hunting trip
with Wata. I have the answer to my question: I *am* the
one-winged pierid. Because of my foot, I too have no
chance to survive in the Amazon. I visualize the injured
butterfly's last moment before death—scramble-crawling
as he tried to get away. I picture myself run-limping.
Similar. Pitiful. Futile.

Looking up, I stop. I'm in a garden. Could it be . . .
could it be the Takunami garden? It looks familiar: the

manioc plants, the maize, the weeded rows of *pu-ni-ka*. My mind races. If it is . . . I *am* close. Maybe . . . maybe . . . maybe . . .

"*Yeow!*"

A familiar tan and black beast slinks out from behind a tree in front of me. The female jaguar.

The low growl of the black jaguar rumbles behind me. I'm surrounded.

Spinning around, I see the black cat inching toward me.

Suddenly I hear the woman's song I had been following earlier on the trail.

Come this way, the voice sings softly but strongly. *Do not be afraid. Open your eyes and come this way.*

I look toward the mottled jaguar. She is staring at me. The song is coming from her. It has been all along.

Come this way. The song continues, the words pulling me forward. *Let go of your body, trust in your soul, open your eyes and come. . . .*

The black cat leaps. One powerful paw slashes my legs from under me and I slam to the ground. The mottled female darts around my body; I hear a grunt as they collide. I scramble to get up, but my right leg collapses. Crab-walking, I scuttle backward. The two cats separate and shadow each other like boxers. Two times they circle.

Then three. With each rotation, they hunker lower, as if their bodies are being screwed into the ground. They watch for that flick of muscle, that telling shift, those hind legs lowering slightly. The movement will be subtle, the following action . . . possibly deadly. Blinking would be risky; looking away could be suicide. But she does. Glancing over the black jaguar's shoulder, the female locks eyes with me.

Go, her stare says. *Go, now.*

In my mind, the gaze lasts a lifetime; in reality, it is a second. It's all he needs. Shrieking, the black cat is on her.

Unable to walk, I crawl along the mud path. Rotting leaves stick to my skin. A fallen tree blocks the path. I turn around to crab-walk over it, but my leg screams as I bend it, and I collapse onto the trunk, gritting my teeth in pain. For the first time, I stop to look at my injury, and I stare in disbelief. My right calf is sliced from the back of the knee to the ankle. Mud has mixed with blood to form a sort of bandage. Since there's nothing I can do, I grit my teeth, turn back to my hands and knees, and keep crawling.

I am like the pathetic five-legged bu-ki ant, dragging myself along.

I will return to the village as I left, I promised myself two days ago at the river. Two days ago when I was strong.

Two days ago when I was stupid. Two days ago, when I was twelve.

The sky is turning that shade of pinkish blue that makes you feel anything is possible. It is a new day. I hear empty water pails being collected and the dry rattling cough of someone's grandfather. I am almost there. My instinct tells me to keep going, my mind tells me to stop, my body is along for the ride.

This is not how it's supposed to happen. I've imagined this moment, meeting my father . . . hundreds, no, thousands of times. In my vision, I was chest-out strong, chin-up proud, and rock solid on two feet. And Paho's face—the one I made up—was at first shocked, then amazed, then ashamed as he stared at me. He would apologize and then want to know how I had done it, all the while showing me off: *Look at my son, Tirio. Do you remember him? He could barely walk when he left and now he is as solid as a po-no.* Laughing, he would shake my legs to prove the point and I would stand there, smiling and nodding. That is the way it was supposed to be. I look down at myself, my skinny body, my dirty clothes, my ravaged leg. A rooster crows in the distance. Not like this. I won't do it. I won't disappoint him again.

LUKA

27 Years, 72 Sunrises
The Amazon

I cannot see Tirio, but I know he is near. Near enough that I could run or yell to him, yet I do not. Talk and touch are not allowed in the soche seche tente until the boy has crossed the village border, so I stand as close as I can and wait. I hear the jaguar scream and feel the thud as the two cats collide.

This is your chance, Tirio. Run! Run fast!

Holding out my hands, I face their direction and channel my energy. I send it through the rivers of rain on the earth, in the breath of the wind tunneling down the path, and with the rays of the rising sun I feel on my face.

He is not resisting me as he has the last two days, and I am worried. A fallen soul sucks a body down faster than a hungry caiman in a death roll. I hope it is not too late.

I have visualized our first meeting many times, but,

having never experienced it with my own paho, there has always been an uncertainty. I knew it would be wonderful, yet strange. We would be overjoyed to finally meet, yet unsure about what to say or do. I imagined we'd stare at each other and compare: same nose, same cheeks, same chin, same smile. We would talk and discover the same voice, same gestures, same laugh.

Now I wonder if the meeting will happen at all.

I open my eyes and stare as something crawls over a fallen log on the trail. Covered in mud and leaves, the creature does not lift its head as it drags along the path. It does not flinch as the branches whip and scratch. It stops, then starts again. Behind me, I hear water buckets being collected and the raspy cough of an elder. The creature hesitates and considers. A rooster crows. The something that is my son crumples. He is a stone's throw away, but it might as well be the moon. I cannot help. He must do it on his own.

Get up, Tirio. Get up, Son.

His mind is foggy. He does not hear me.

Do not give up.

Nothing.

GET UP! NOW!

No response.

I watch him and refuse to blink, in fear that I will miss

a movement. But there is none.

I slide down against the po-no tree and drop my head into my hands. How cruel the Good Gods are to let us get this close.

Hearing a twig snap, I look up. Tirio is crawling again. Seeing the determination in his weak movements, I pound the earth between us.

Yes! Almost there! Five more pulls!

He doesn't look up, but I know he can feel the vibrations.

ONE!

TWO!

THREE!

FOUR!

FIVE!

He grasps my hand and collapses. His eyes are closed, but he is breathing. I am shaking so badly, I almost do not trust myself, but I grab under his knees and arms and stumble toward the village. Blood is dripping down my arms and I am scared because I do not know where it is coming from.

"Do not die," I sob. "Please do not die."

He tenses at the sound of my voice and then goes limp. I freeze. My eyes dart between his lips and his chest.

What happened? Is he still breathing? Feeling his heartbeat against my forearm, I pull him close and sprint the rest of the way to my hut. Easing him onto my sister's hammock, I scream for her. "Sulali!"

She rushes in and I explain what happened.

"Go to the *ku-mah-kah* tree," she says, handing me two covered baskets. "Fill these with ants. Run."

I am there and back before the shadows have shortened a hair. "How is he? Is he still alive?"

"He will be fine. I stopped the bleeding." Sulali finishes cleaning the wound. "The cut is deep, but it is straight and will heal well. We must hurry, Luka." She motions for me to sit. "I want to finish before he wakes."

Unlatching the top of a basket, I seize one of the giant *qu-qu-lola* ants. Twisting around, it snaps at me with pincers the size of a child's finger. Sulali squeezes the edges of Tirio's wound, and I place the insect next to the flesh. The ant digs into the two pieces of skin, pulling them together. My sister swiftly slices the body off with a knife and then tugs on the leftover head and jaws. The seam of skin lifts and pulls, but holds together. She nods, satisfied.

We work quickly. I position each insect. It pinches angrily. Sulali chops and checks for a tight hold. Forty ants later, we are finished. Sulali sweeps the writhing remains out the door, where our pet *yanuti* squawks and pecks excitedly at the unexpected free meal.

I stare at the tidy row of ant mandibles that seal the wound. If only Tirio and I can heal our relationship that neatly.

CHAPTER ELEVEN

TIRIO

13 Years
The Amazon

"Tirio . . ."

It is the familiar voice of my father, the man I have heard more from in the last two days than in the past thirteen years of my life.

"Son, wake up," he says.

It is the same voice, yet different.

Someone shakes my shoulders, and the ground underneath me sways strangely. Where am I? I struggle to swim through my exhaustion to the surface of consciousness. Am I dead? Forcing my heavy eyelids open a slit, I see the bottom half of my body. It is covered with a large *turunu* tree leaf, and beyond that a thick vine reaches out and wraps around a tall vertical pole. I'm lying in a hammock in someone's hut. Whose hut? His? Without moving my head, I slowly scan both directions. To my right, a fire burns; small leaf-wrapped bundles circle it, the contents inside slowly cooking on the warm coals. A pair of tree stumps sit side by side, their tops worn smooth by repeated use as stools. To my left hangs another hammock, and then behind it smaller ones, suspended between poles, filled with fruit, vegetables, and dried meat—the Takunami version of shelves.

"Tirio?" My father sounds scared.

I open my eyes a little more. On each side of my body, long brown arms cage me in.

I now realize why his voice sounds different. It's outside my head, not inside. My gaze follows a long blue vein snaking down the inside of his elbow to his clenched hand gripping the edge of my hammock.

"Tirio, can you see me?" Calloused fingers lift my chin, but I keep my eyes down. I'm not ready to look at him yet.

Outside, boys laugh and sticks strike each other with solid *whacks*. War cries are whooped and then suddenly stop. A man's angry whispers fill the silence, and tentative footsteps creep by. A little girl sings and claps her hands until an older woman shushes her and she quiets. *Umutinas* call out to each other, echoing and then adding on to their mate's caw. Then, even they fade off into the distance. Except for the occasional crack of the fire, total silence surrounds us. It is as though the universe is waiting

178

for this moment . . . this reunion between us. *Stop watching us!* I want to yell. *Go away.* I don't know what to do. I don't know what to say. This is not how it was supposed to be!

I keep staring at the vein in my father's arm and imagine the blood pulsing through it. It's the same blood that's coursing through me right now. He leans down. "You made it. You are safe," he says.

I allow myself to look up at his mouth, but no higher. He runs his tongue over his lips nervously and I see where they are cracked in several places. *I have dry lips too,* I think, and then scold myself. *A lot of people have chapped lips, stupid. That's not something dads genetically share with their sons.*

Is it?

"Do you understand me, Son?" The muscles in his jaw tense. "Tirio, say something."

I close my eyes and swallow.

"Tirio!"

"Whh . . ." It comes out as a croak. I clear my throat. "Why?"

He lets out a sigh of relief after hearing my voice and straightens up.

"Why?" I say again. "Why did you give up?"

"Give up?" He sounds confused. "I didn't give up. I

kept trying to communicate, but you wouldn't listen."

I continue to keep my eyes down. If I just keep imagining him the way I have for the past thirteen years, I won't fall apart. "No, not yesterday. When I was six. Why did you give up on me?"

My father drags to the window like a prisoner with a ball and chain. His legs and feet are muddy, but his muscles move powerfully under his brown skin. His strength doesn't surprise me; I never expected him to share my disability. Yet something about seeing him walk without any problem revives the anger I've always felt for him.

When he doesn't answer, I snort. "Even now you won't admit the truth—that you were ashamed of me."

"I wasn't ashamed," he begins. "You were very young when you left, Tirio. It's not—"

"You wanted me dead," I interrupt, accusing him with my words. "You didn't think I was strong enough to be a Takunami warrior. You didn't want me."

In the long silence that follows, I let myself look up at his torso. His shoulders are slumped and he's buried his face in his hands. His fingers cover his eyes. Long fingers . . . just like mine.

Slowly he removes his hands and I freeze in shock. He looks just like me. Except older, but not by much— maybe fifteen years. He's got my nose and my eyes, my lopsided frown. I shift to see the side of his face; he's even got my pinned-back ears. He's so young. He looks like my brother, not my father.

"Is that what you thought all these years?" he asks quietly. "My son, there are many things you do not understand."

"Tell me." I blink back tears. "What don't I understand?"

The sadness in his eyes scares me. They're the only part of his face that looks old. "Your maha thought she was doing the right thing that day. She . . ."

Maha! I sit up and gasp as pain shoots through my leg.

"Tirio, do not move." He rushes toward me. "You might open the wound."

"Where's Maha?"

Why did he just look down? My mouth goes dry.

"I should start at the beginning," he says.

"Where is she?" My calf is on fire, and the tears flow freely now.

There is a long silence before he finally speaks. "She's dead, Tirio."

"You're lying."

He shakes his head.

I don't respond. I can't. Her last words to me echo in my head: *I too will pay.*

181

My father squats close to me. "The whole thing was a mistake . . . a misunderstanding."

Numbly, I listen as he speaks about his childhood: his mother and Sulali, Karara and Tukkita, Kiwano and the Punhana and then finally Maroma.

"Since I never took the soche seche tente, I could not be considered a Takunami man, and the tribe was unsure what to do. Tukkita consulted the spirits, and they told him I would be given another chance. But the test would be more difficult—and this time, it would include my son. The visions said that at six years old you should be sent away to live with the Vanaalas."

My eyes widen. A Takunami sent to live with another tribe?

"We are at peace with them. You would not have been harmed," he assures me, reading my mind. "Two days before your thirteenth birthday, you were to be told the truth and taken into the jungle. Using the sixth sense, I was to bring you back to our village. Only then would we both be Takunami men."

I sit there, unable to speak.

"I did not want to send you away." His eyes plead with me to understand. "At first, I told Tukkita no. I would sacrifice my own life before giving you up to the

Vanaalas for so long. But I was thinking with my heart and not my head. If I was dead, you would be left without a guide for your soche seche tente. Tukkita did not think the spirits would look kindly on my selfishness and would punish you and Maroma. I had no choice but to pray for time to pass quickly and then bring you back on your birthday."

A laugh of relief escapes through my tears. "So it didn't matter that I had a bad foot?"

"Never. In fact, I think the Good Gods wounded you to make things harder for me. But Maroma blamed herself. She knew your importance to our family, so she tried to hide your weakness until she could fix it."

I nod. "She used to carry me everywhere when we were in the village, but then after we finished our work, she'd take me out to the jungle and make me walk until I collapsed."

"Your body always gave out before your spirit did," my father says. "You had the same determination the last few days as you did when you were a little boy many moons ago with Maroma." He crosses his arms. "I'm glad to see you did not lose it. Even if it meant you refused to listen to anything I said."

I look down, my face growing hot. "I didn't know. . . ."

"It's fine," he says. "Maroma was the same way . . . stubborn."

There's a moment of silence, and I can see that my father is thinking of her too.

"She tried everything: ointments, chanting, even offering her foot to the evil spirits if they got out of yours," he said. "And she got very frustrated when nothing worked, so she went to Tukkita. The shaman, knowing the Good Gods' plan, assured her of your safety. At first she believed him, but after seeing others stare and whisper, she became nervous. She heard Tukkita tell me it was time for you to go."

His earlier words echo in my head. *The whole thing was a mistake . . . a misunderstanding.* I clutch my head. "She thought you were going to kill me?" I say in disbelief.

My father runs his fingers through his hair. "Yes."

"Why didn't you tell her the truth?"

"I did not tell anyone. I was afraid you might find out. If I lost this second chance to pass the test, the spirits would not have given me another. After what happened with my paho, our family would have appeared cursed."

I look away, knowing we would have been asked to leave the tribe. He had been protecting all of us.

His voice lowers as he continues explaining things to

me. "When a Takunami is killed by his tribe, his soul is poisoned, which makes it unable to enter any plants or animals. It floats around forever without a home. Maroma put you in a *suwata curara*, to let the spirit of the river decide what should happen to you. She hoped that if you were to die, at least your spirit would be saved.

"When she returned to the village, she told everyone that you had been playing in the water and were dragged under by an anaconda. People believed her story because she was so upset, but I remembered the vision I had of you in the suwata curara and confronted her. She admitted the truth." He looks away. "Three days later we found her . . ."

No! Like a newly released ball in a pinball machine, the word ricochets against every organ in my body. *Bang*— my stomach. *Bang*—my heart. *Bang*—my brain. By the time it gets to my tongue and I try to spit it out, he's already started speaking again.

". . . floating in the wash area. She had tied her hands and feet and thrown herself from a canoe."

"But it wasn't her fault!" I cry. "She didn't know."

"She did not know because I did not tell her." From his eyelids to his knees, my father wears his guilt like a heavy stone cloak.

His words swirl around me as the mystery of my life

185

unravels. Resentment built by my imagination wrestles with reality.

"So all this time, you've been waiting for me to turn thirteen so you could be considered a man?" I ask.

He shakes his head. "No. All this time I've been waiting for you to turn thirteen so *you* could be considered a man."

"Why?"

"Three people died because of me, Tirio. First Paho because he ingested all the male spirits so I could be born, and then Maroma killed herself because I didn't tell her the truth, and lastly Karara, after I lied about not finding her that day of my scent test."

"Karara died?" I ask.

He nods. "For several moons after my father's funeral, she snuck into the village at night and secretly visited Tukkita. Then one time, after she left his hut, Tukkita heard her scream mixed with the scream of a jaguar. We ran out to help her, but all we found on the trail were her footsteps and then the tracks of the cat." He shakes his head. "She never visited Tukkita again."

"I'm sorry," I say softly.

He leans his elbows on his knees and stares me straight in the eye. "That's why it's so important that you're here. You are the only one who lived, in spite of me. Yes, you needed to pass your soche seche tente before I could become a warrior, but for the past thirteen years, I've wanted nothing more than this moment—for you to be sitting in front of me, alive and strong." He grabs my hands. "And you are strong, Tirio, stronger in ways I will never be."

For the past seven years, those words ruled my life. I wanted to hear them. I *needed* to hear them. Now as I look at my father, I realize they've ruled his life too.

LUKA

27 Years, 72 Sunrises
The Amazon

The sun and the moon are the only company Tirio and I have as we catch up on forty years of living: thirteen years of his life, plus twenty-seven of mine.

He is a different boy from the one I carried out of the woods this morning. His eyes are clear and he barely stops for a breath as he tells me about soccer, Sara, and his friend Joey. He tears hungrily at the dried meat I give him and he laughs so loud that I jump when he speaks about an elder named Cal who cooks soup. I smile and nod, staring at the person Maroma and I created. My son.

He has stopped talking and I am about to ask how his leg feels when he suddenly asks me a question.

"When I was little, what did you think when you saw me, limping and hobbling around the village? Did you wish that another boy was your son?" He looks down at the ground and whispers, "Were you ashamed?"

I offer him some dried papaya. He takes it.

"I felt a lot of things: sadness that you had to be kept from the other children, anger at the Good Gods for punishing my family again, and helplessness because I couldn't do anything. But no, Tirio, *never, ever* did I feel ashamed of you."

Tirio finishes eating and I scoop some more water out of the barrel and pour it into his cup.

"I was worried at first," I admit. "Like Maroma, I was nervous about what the tribe might want to do with you."

"That they might want me dead?"

"Most sick babies are killed soon after they are born."

"So why wasn't I?"

"You were born under a lucky moon, Tirio. She was full the night you came into this world. Maroma held on to you long enough to make it so, and I believe the two of them watched over you. Your two mothers—the moon and Maroma—protected you."

At first Tirio doesn't say anything, but his face looks sad. I quickly continue.

"When Maroma could do nothing more for you, she passed you on to another female spirit—the river. You should have died, but the river took you in as her child also. She rocked, cradled, and protected you from even the worst of herself. So, really, you have three mothers."

So many emotions cross Tirio's face, and I pause to let him sort things through. When he finally speaks, it is almost a whisper: "And when the Amazon couldn't do anything more, she passed me on to Sara."

Silently, I nod. "Yes . . . four mothers." I think about my own maha living only a few huts away. We have not spoken in many sunrises. "As I said . . . you are lucky."

"I used to think you could only have one," my son says softly. "I didn't want to replace Maha."

"She would have been happy to know someone was taking care of you," I tell him.

He lifts his leg up carefully and leans back in my hammock. "When I was out in the jungle, I heard a woman singing. I was hoping it was her," he admits.

I bow my head. "I'm sorry, Tirio. Only shaman spirits can be heard by the living."

"Then who was it? It was the first afternoon, and she kept singing 'Come this way. Do not be afraid. Open your eyes and come this way.'"

"I don't know," I say, shaking my head.

"And then later the female jaguar seemed to be singing the same song."

I freeze as the pieces click into place: the story I told

Sulali about Karara and the Punhana, my sister with her head thrown back wailing at Paho's funeral, the jaguar helping Tirio.

I put down my cup and rise to my feet. "I have to go."

My son's eyes flicker nervously around the hut.

"You will be safe," I assure him. "I won't be long."

As I race to the garden, I know she will be there. Just as she was the night before I was supposed to take my soche seche tente. I go to the spot where Maha and I left her crying on the ground.

"Karara?" I speak in the darkness.

The night animals quiet and we wait for her response together.

She is here. I can feel her.

"I am sorry." My words slice the night air.

She is behind me, but I do not face her. Not yet.

"It was my fault," I add.

Hearing the rustling of leaves, I turn. She steps into the glow of the moonlight and, even though she is my sister, I dare not get closer. Her neck is bleeding and her eyes are tired.

"He made it," I tell her.

I can almost see her smile.

"Thank you, Karara."

She blinks.

"Thank you for bringing the boy home."

Neither of us moves. We stare at each other in silence.

Finally she looks past me toward the village. *Go to him*, the look says. *Go*.

I nod and start toward the path. When I glance back, the moonlight illuminates an empty clearing.

The jaguar is gone.

CHAPTER TWELVE

TIRIO

13 Years, 1 Sunrise
The Amazon

I fell sound asleep as soon as my father left. The last thing I remember is swinging my uninjured leg out of the hammock and listening to the hushed sounds of the village getting ready for bed. An anaconda could have slithered into the hut and swallowed me whole and I wouldn't have realized until I woke up in its belly the next morning.

"Drink," Paho says when I finally open my eyes. He helps me into a sitting position and hands me some tea. "For your leg."

I take a sip and cringe at the bitterness. My father hands me some honey. "You can escape from a hungry jaguar yet you cannot drink tea without honey?" he teases.

I hear the clanging of pots outside and two women talking. I think of Sara and my heart sinks. I'm sure she's still looking for me. She won't stop until they find me . . .

or my body. "How long did I sleep?"

"The sun is now midsky."

I do the math in my head. I've been gone three and a half days. She must be crazy with worry.

Glancing down at my leg, I see it's been bandaged with a po-no leaf and crisscrossed with vines. I look like I'm wearing Roman gladiator boots.

"Sulali covered it while you were asleep. To keep the flies off," my father explains. He nods behind me. "She figured you might try to walk today."

Leaning up on my elbow, I turn around. A wide-eyed young woman, not much older than me, steps hesitantly into view. Gliding over, she kisses me on the forehead, a traditional greeting for nonmarried family members. A single long braid of hair falls over her shoulder as she leans down. She pulls it carefully out of the way. "Congratulations on becoming a warrior," she says in a soft voice.

"I don't feel like much of a warrior right now," I laugh. "But *shu-u-we*. Thank you. And thank you for what you did." I motion to my injury. "My father told me that you're really good with helping sick people."

The reed door is pushed open roughly and we all jump in surprise. I stare at the serious-looking man who stomps into the room. His eyelids are rimmed in red and his fists clench and unclench at his sides until he hides them behind his back. I look to my father, but he doesn't seem worried, so I relax.

"It is good to have you back," the man says. He looks familiar. Why?

"Tirio, this is our shaman, Kiwano," Paho says. "He took over after Tukkita died."

Kiwano! The name registers in my head. That's why I recognize him. He was the only other Takunami boy who did not climb trees besides me, when I was younger. Maha had whispered that it was because he had seen the Punhana when he was in a tree, and after that he refused to ever go up a tree again.

I stare at him now, shocked at how old he looks. Older than my father, yet I know he is much younger.

He shifts his gaze away from my surprised face and speaks to the wall. "The tribe has been told of your journey," he explains, "and they would like to hold a celebration in your honor—and Luka's as well. A double soche seche tente celebration."

I grin, and so does my paho. When we look at each other we both start laughing.

Kiwano shakes his head and strides toward the door.

"Tonight, the feast of the warriors. We will welcome you into the tribe as the men you have proven yourselves to be." He grunts and leaves.

We immediately start preparing. Sulali brings us some gi-gi berries, and my father and I paint each other's faces red. I have dreamed of wearing this mask many times, and now it is finally happening. My smiling face does not match that of a ferocious warrior, but I don't care. I couldn't hide my excitement with the dye from a million gi-gi berries.

I ask for another po-no leaf and attempt to decorate my right leg so that it matches my left. After watching my struggles, Sulali sighs and pushes me gently aside. She rolls her braid up into a bun and skillfully mimics the look exactly, then does the same for my father when he asks.

"I like it," he says, strutting around the hut.

I give him the thumbs-up and then have to explain what it means.

He hands me some white feathers from the *ikulu* bird and we use *rioba* sap to attach them to our hair. This tradition is a show of respect for the Good Gods, thanking them for allowing us make it to this point in our journey of life. It's also a request for continued protection in our new roles as warriors. The white feathers are the most important decoration of all and I add extra, hoping to show that I realize how much the Good Gods helped me.

Takunami males are born three times: once out of their mahas' bodies into the world, once out of their boyhood bodies into manhood, and once out of their physical bodies into the spirit world. We enter each phase as we entered the first one—naked. As I strip down now to my skin, I truly feel as though I'm shedding everything from my past and starting new.

Bam, bam, bam, bam. Pause. *Bam, bam, bam, bam.* Pause. *Bam.*

The beating of the drums calls us out. Trying not to lean too heavily against my paho, I limp down the path and into the circle of women and children. A young boy touches the back of my leg and I jump. His mother slaps his hand and hisses a warning. I grit my teeth in pain but manage a smile, and they both quickly lower their eyes.

Kiwano waits for us by the fire, and after we take our seats on two carved stools in the center, I scan the circle of brown eyes staring at me. The women look at me with respect and the children with awe. I lift my chin and clench my jaw. For the first time, I see myself as everyone else does—as a Takunami man. Kiwano pounds his staff and lets out a long, low wail. The women begin yipping and yapping and the men sneak in on tiptoes from the shadows. In twos they run toward us. As soon as their feet enter the circle, they begin dancing as if their souls are on fire and the only way to stamp it out is through their feet. Although I am able to maintain the stern face of the warrior, inside a little part of me is yipping, yapping, screaming, singing, and dancing too.

While Kiwano is placing the strings of black warrior beads around our necks, I see a woman in the circle duck her head and peer over her shoulder toward the forest. She is the only one not transfixed by what is going on in front of her.

A feast is served, and Paho and I are honored with the best of everything. The most tender parts of the peccary, the coveted eggs of the *torucha* turtle, and the rare *boquri* fruit are all piled high on large, flat pieces of manioc bread and served to us by Vaku, the latest boy who became a warrior. It will be our responsibility to serve the next warrior.

I eat like a person who's been out in the jungle for two days, shoving way too much food in my mouth and only stopping to blurt out *shu-u-we* to the line of people laying gifts of arrows, dye, and spears in front of us. The whole time, I continue to watch the woman closely.

After Vaku brings me my second helping, I pause and

turn toward my father. "What is she looking for?" I ask him, nodding in the woman's direction.

He puts down the bone he is gnawing on and motions toward the blackness of the forest.

"Her eldest son is out there."

"He's taking his soche seche tente right now?"

My father nods.

I stare at the woman. She hasn't touched her food, yet every time she looks away, the old woman sitting next to her reaches out a gnarled hand and picks at it. I want to assure her that her son will be fine, that he will return alive. I want her to enjoy the ceremony, so I can too.

After the food, there is more celebrating and everyone is dancing: the women, the children, even the pet parrots bob their heads to the drumbeats. I keep thinking about Sara.

I tap my father on the arm.

"I have to go," I say.

LUKA

27 Years, 73–74 Sunrises
The Amazon

I am not ready to lose Tirio again so quickly.

"What about your leg?" I ask, motioning to his wound. "You cannot walk like that."

"Can I take one of your canoes?" he asks. "Just to get me back to my boat?"

I remember the night Tukkita and I consulted the Good Gods, the night I saw the vision of a six-year-old Tirio alone in a suwata curara being pulled away from me by the river. It is not something I want to experience again.

"One man cannot make it paddling against the current. I will go with you."

He grabs my arm. "No, Paho. The Takunami are a secret and they must remain that way," he says. "I just need you to help me get to my boat. It has a motor."

Motor? I do not know the word.

He shakes his head and laughs. "It's not important.

200

But just know I'll be fine."

A group of children circle us and start singing a song.

"*Shu-u-we*." Tirio smiles and claps when they finish. Giggling and pushing, they scatter away.

"I'm sorry," he says. "I don't want to leave all this. There is still so much I need to do: go hunting and fishing with you, move into the men's rohacas together . . ." He turns toward the worried mother still staring out into the darkness. "I want to stay and see her son stumble into the village, exhausted but successful in a couple of days and be the one to serve him his celebratory meal." He pauses. "But I can't."

His eyes look into mine, and I can see by the crease between them that he's not asking for approval. He's asking for understanding.

I nod, and with my next words I hope I give him both. "You are a man now," I say. "You must take care of your family."

The lines on his face relax. "*Shu-u-we*, Paho."

"We can leave with the sunrise." I hand him a cup of fustitu. "Now let's return to celebrating your success."

"*Our* success," he corrects me.

I drink half of my cup and then throw the rest on the fire as an offering to the Good Gods. Tirio does the same. The fire hisses and dims but then flares up high into the night sky. The black ash turns gray as it rises and fattens into clouds. I tilt my head to watch the smoke form shapes and float toward the moon, like children being called home.

The next morning, as soon as it is light enough to see, Tirio and I head for the river. Some of the men grunt their good-byes as we leave the men's rohacas, others look away, angry that such a strong warrior is allowed to leave the tribe.

Kiwano gave his blessing last night. "The Good Gods approve," he said after staring into the fire for a long time. He then shoved his staff into Tirio's hand.

"It is filled with healing spirits," he promised gruffly. "If you are not going to let me help you properly, it is the best I can do." He then turned and disappeared in the darkness toward his hut.

Sulali comes running up to us now, gasping for breath, and hands Tirio a couple of leaves. "Here are some things to help with your pain," she says. "I'm not a shaman, but my sister was very generous with her knowledge when she used to have to watch me. I wanted to get them fresh this morning."

"We must go now, Sulali," I say. "I will return soon."

202

She leans in and kisses Tirio on the forehead before heading back toward the village, her newly braided hair swinging in eight separate sections along her back.

When we get to the wash area, the sun is still only halfway visible above the river, and out of habit I stop to make sure the gate is closed. By the time I turn around, Tirio is already lowering himself carefully into the canoe, chewing on one of the leaves Sulali gave him. He is even stronger than I had thought. As I push the boat off, I tell him that we are going to stay close to the bank.

"The river is weaker here and we are hidden," I explain.

In response, he nods and starts paddling strongly on the left side of the boat.

Watching the muscles in his back work, I feel a surge of pride and match my pull rhythm with his. The boat surges forward, the river letting us glide along easily, as if she understands that this is the last time I'm going to have a moment like this.

By midday we reach the caiman den. Tirio holds up his hand, motioning me to stop, but I continue paddling. There are two boats on the beach ahead, and I hear a man and woman speaking.

"I am going to stay with you until the end, Tirio," I

whisper. "Please. Allow me this one last thing."

Again, he only nods.

I keep the canoe close to the jungle, allowing Tirio and me to sneak up on the couple and see them before they see us. They are on the other side of a shelter, bent over something, arguing, and do not even hear me help Tirio out.

We stand and stare at each other for a moment, until he finally reaches out and hugs me.

I feel his heart beating against my chest. Or maybe it's mine beating against his. I cannot tell.

Kuiju, my son, I think.

I love you too, Paho, he replies. *I love you too.*

Still unnoticed, we pull apart. Holding two fingers in front of his lips, Tirio motions me away.

I climb into the canoe and push off. After Maroma died, I grew to hate the Amazon—all it did was take people from me. Now as I paddle home, I forgive the river. At least once, she brought someone back.

I now know who my son is. He is a man with a strong soul but a wound in his body. I am the opposite. I am a man with a strong body but a wound in my soul. By passing our soche seche tente, Tirio and I have earned the honor of being called warriors. And warriors leave the scars of their boyhood behind them.

Tirio is alive and his spirit is safe. Maroma and I did our jobs. The past seven years and so many deaths were not wasted. I must let him go.

Tonight when I return to the village, Kiwano will consult the Good Gods. They will choose a second wife for me, and in a few sunsets we will get married. We will try for a son. I will never forget Maroma or Tirio, but I must move on. I must survive. It is the way of the Takunami.

EPILOGUE

TIRIO

13 Years, 2 Sunrises

"Tirio!" Sara runs up, pulling me into a hug. "Oh my God, you're alive! How did you get here? Where have you been? We've been searching all over for you."

Juan Diego stands behind her and gives me a little wave.

"I'm fine, Sara," I say, squeezing her tightly. "Really. I went back to my village, like I said in my note. I'm sorry you were worried, but I had to do this."

"Do what?" she asks, letting me go. "The test you wrote about?"

I nod. "My soche seche tente. I had to try, Sara." I say the words I'd been practicing in the canoe. "It was my birthday and I was getting these messages, we were going to be here anyway, so—"

Juan Diego holds a finger to his lips, and I break off in midsentence.

Sara puts her hands on her hips and stares off into the jungle. I look to Juan Diego for help, but he just shoots me a patient smile.

When Sara finally speaks, her voice is soft. "Did you pass?" she asks.

It is not the response I expected and it takes me a minute to answer. "Yes. I did." I pause. "But then I told them I wanted to come back home."

She closes her eyes and drops her chin to her chest. When her body starts to shudder, I realize she's crying.

"Sara . . ." I limp over to her.

"I'm just so glad you're okay." She turns and hugs me again. "Whatever reason you needed to leave, we'll deal with later, but for now, I'm just glad you're alive and that you're here."

"Me too," I whisper. "Me too."

She pulls away, noticing the bandage of leaves. "What's that?" She sniffles.

I look down at my leg. "Oh. I got attacked by a jaguar," I say.

"Of course you did." She throws back her head and laughs.

When I don't join her, she realizes I'm not kidding. Shaking her head, she sighs and puts her arm around me. "And this coming from someone who, less than a week ago, wanted to be normal, *just like everyone else*."

A clatter of metal causes us both to turn. Juan Diego is breaking down the tent.

He peeks around the collapsed rain flap. "I figure we might want to head back to the camp now. Have someone look at Tirio's wound, take a shower . . ." He pats his belly. "Eat some lunch."

"Sounds perfect," I reply. "Table for three, please."

In the days that follow, I'm unable to do any of the things that Sara and I had planned: visit the tribes, learn to dance—certainly not climb a kapok. Not with my leg. Not this time. But at night when we sit on the porch together, I do manage to gain Sara's forgiveness by explaining everything that happened to me. It helps that she's an anthropologist and is used to dealing with the customs of jungle tribes. In order to prove myself, I admit to showing off a little.

"Do you hear that?" I say on the night before we're supposed to leave. "That *kee-kee-ka*? That's a *yulano*—a tiny yellow cricket. And that other sound? That's the flapping of the wings of the *kuipa,* the bat that's going to eat the yulano."

When the *kee-kee-ka* stops suddenly, Sara raises her

eyebrows in surprise. "Wow. You are good. And what's that whooshing sound that just went by?"

"A *humgura*."

"And the croaking to our right?"

"An *ikina*."

"And that rumbling?"

"That's my stomach," I joke.

"Ha-ha." She punches me lightly on the shoulder and then stretches. "I'm heading to bed, Tirio."

"Okay," I say, suddenly distracted by a sound I just picked up. Padded footsteps.

"You're not going to take off again, are you?" she asks sarcastically, holding open the door.

"No, no," I say, standing. Deep breathing. Could it be? I follow her inside.

Lying in bed, I focus my energy on blocking everything out but the sound of the approaching animal. It is her. Right outside the perimeter of the research camp, the female jaguar stops, climbs a tree, and begins to purr.

When we get back to Miami, Joey's dad has moved into an apartment a few blocks from Sara and me.

"He promised to take me on some of his flights this

summer," Joey says excitedly, stretching in preparation for our championship game. "California, New York, maybe even an international one."

I just nod and pick at the rubber on my crutches, not mentioning that the game starts in five minutes and there's no sign of his father. Just as the referee blows the whistle and Joey takes my place as goalie, Mr. Carter's black Mercedes pulls up. He runs up next to me on the sidelines and whistles loudly, calling out Joey's name. Joey grins and waves.

Mr. Carter turns to me. "Hey, Tirio. How's the leg?"

"Fine, Mr. Carter," I say. "Thanks." After a pause, I add, "I'm glad you made it."

"Me too," he says before looking back toward the action and calling out words of encouragement to his son.

He seems to really mean it.

Even though I only knew him for a short time, I miss my paho. We still communicate. At dawn or dusk, I sometimes hear the howler monkeys claiming their territory, and last week I smelled fresh papaya in the middle of my algebra exam. It's the only time I've ever smiled during a test.

In return, I send him feelings I think he'll enjoy, like the thrill of taking off in an airplane, the rush of riding a bike down a steep hill, and the taste of Cal's soup du jour.

My name is Tirio and I am thirteen years old. I am a man. I am a son. I am a Takunami warrior.

AUTHOR'S NOTE

S cientists believe there are tribes in the rain forest we know nothing about. The Takunami tribe is imaginary, as are all of its rituals. They are based on an idea, and not on a representation of any known Amazonian people. All of the book's characters are fictional, and although a number of the plants and animals mentioned in the text really do exist in the Amazon jungle, others do not. Some of the words spoken by the Takunami are used by certain Amazonian people, but much of the language is made up.

The idea for this story came from an experience I had while staying at a remote research camp in Brazil. On my second night there, I developed a stomachache and asked our guide, Juan Diego, for some local medicine. He enlisted the help of the cook, who went into the woods, gathered some leaves, and brewed a mild, green-colored tea. Amazed at my recovery, I requested the name of the plant, so I could buy more tea when we got back to town. Juan Diego told me the name, but explained that five minutes down the river, the tribe there would call it something else. The power of plants and the diversity of the jungle people stayed with me and "steeped" for two years before becoming the seed of *Bringing the Boy Home*.

ACKNOWLEDGMENTS

I owe the people below a tremendous amount of gratitude:

My three favorite English teachers: Mary Sue Mordica, Linda Wityk, and Barbara M. Epstein. You planted and nurtured a seed of hope in a young girl many years ago, and look what it has become. I'm so happy to be able to share this with you.

My family: Mom for allowing me to be bored enough during summer vacation that I was forced to figure out what I really love to do. Dad, for always having a nightstand full of books and for dropping me off at the Fort Leonard Wood library before I was old enough to drive. Katja and George, for being the best sister and brother a person stuck out in the middle of nowhere could ask for. Danielle, for encouraging me to pursue every dream I've ever had; your anguish at the wind blowing my manuscript into the lake was the best compliment I could have received.

The members of my critique groups, especially Amanda Marrone, for telling me when my writing was good—and also very, very bad.

My three editors: Leann Heywood, for believing in *Bringing the Boy Home* enough to fight for it to win the Ursula Nordstrom contest. Rachel Orr, for adopting the story (and me) and being so patient with my novice ignorance. Adriana Dominguez, for being the rock-solid anchor of this long-distance race and pulling the novel through the final stages even though your publishing plate was already "Thanksgiving Day" full.

And lastly, the people I share my life with every day: Rafferty, for giving me pregnancy-induced insomnia and a place to put my laptop from midnight until four o'clock in the morning while you kept me up. Soleil and Abby, for being as good as I could expect a two-year-old and a hunting dog to be during long walks through the woods in which I tried to clear my head. And lastly, John, my teammate and husband, who, no matter what kind of chaos life was throwing our way, never failed to make the world shut up long enough to look me in the eye and ask, "What can I do to help?"

You did it, honey.

Thank you, all.